Dedication

To John and Susan, and Melinda and Jim.
And to all the fans who asked when I'd finish this one.
This is for you.

It Came to Tranquility

Tracy S. Morris

It Came to Tranquility
Tracy S. Morris
First Edition Copyright © Tracy S. Morris, 2019

Published by Yard Dog Press at Kindle

Print Version ISBN 978-1-945941-20-7
It Came to Tranquility
First Edition Copyright © Tracy S. Morris, 2019

Yard Dog Press
710 W. Redbud Lane
Alma, AR 72921-7247

http://www.yarddogpress.com

Edited by Selina Rosen
Copy & Technical Editor Lynn Rosen
Cover art by Brad W. Foster

First Print Edition September 15, 2019
Printed in the United States of America
0 9 8 7 6 5 4 3 2 1

Table of Contents

Chapter 1: Now

Jake turned off the motor of his police cruiser and sighed as he looked through the windshield. Dr. Dave's beat up car sat in its customary spot next to the old, broken rock fountain, yet no light illuminated the stained glass window of Tranquility Medical.

No sense putting this off, he thought. The front door of the clinic slid open when he tried it. Inside, Dr. Dave sat on an exam table with his head down, a twisted stethoscope dangled from his fingers.

"Doc?"

Dr. Dave stiffened and then peered up at Jake with a wooden expression. "You here to take me in, Jake?"

Jake raked his fingers through his hair. "I gotta' do my job, Doc," he said. "Your ex-fiancée vanished and you're the prime suspect."

"Everyone she knew thought about killing her. Jody rubbed everyone the wrong way."

"Yeah, but you're the only one who doesn't have an alibi," Jake said. "Please don't make this hard on me, Doc. I don't think you did it. I'm I'll clear you soon."

Dr. Dave nodded in a defeated gesture. "Well, I didn't touch her, so the sooner you clear me, the better."

As Jake led the Doc to his squad car, he wracked his brain for any angle in this case he might have missed.

Tracy S. Morris

Chapter 2: Four Months Ago

A thickish layer of ice glazed Lake Tranquility like the frosting on a jelly doughnut. Jake could see it all from his vantage point at the top of the dam's outflow valve. The surface seemed solid, but within the hour the air would fill with the creaks and groans of splitting ice.

Anyone from up North would know those sounds; familiar in spring when the ice thawed, but strange during January in Arkansas. Ice covered lakes like the one below didn't occur here unless they underwent a century freeze like the kind going on right now.

At the sound of footfalls behind him, Jake turned to see Dr. David Nye approach slowly, picking his way along the icy trail.

"Aren't you supposed to be down at the ceremony?" Jake asked.

He almost missed the sour expression Dr. Dave shot him thanks to the heavy wool hood of his coat. The Doc looked like one of Jake's wife Rachel's veterinary patients under all the layers of sweaters and synthetic fur-covered coats he wore.

"Who gave Horace Jones a microphone? Once he has it, he never shuts up!"

"We didn't have much choice, him being Mayor and all," Jake said.

Dr. Dave laughed at that. "You know how a fox will chew off a paw to get out of a snare? I know just how it feels."

"Trapped. Just like me in this monkey suit." Jake tugged at the tie of his stiff, barely-used Tranquility-issue policeman's uniform. "Where are the reporters? I want to get this over with."

"The press conference just broke up," Dr. Dave said. "Rachel got stuck talking to the Walters kid and sent me to tell you."

Jake scoffed. "She's better than that at dodging him."

3

"My guess, pregnancy has messed with her agility," Dr. Dave said. "You should file a restraining order before this is all dry lakebed. Otherwise you'll never get rid of him." He made a sweeping gesture at the ice.

Jake nodded in agreement. Every six months Scott drove into Tranquility searching for treasure. For the past few years, he focused on some fabled hoard Rachel's great-grandfather Coin was said to have buried somewhere in the mountains surrounding his resort. In between semesters Scott badgered Rachel into examining a fictitious treasure map he'd bought off of some con artist. Jake might have worried about Rachel's safety, except that Scott was afraid of Rachel's pet ferrets.

"I can always throw a weasel on him. It worked last time," Jake said.

"Rachel told me you might say that. She said: tell him to behave. Horace worked hard on this ceremony and we don't need your luck to make a boulder fall on Scott Walters like he was Wile E. Coyote."

Jake pushed thoughts of Rachel's stalker aside and patted the controls for the outflow valve. "I know what I'm supposed to do. I keep my trap shut and turn the wheel. 'sides, those reporters'll be too busy watching water leave the lake to pay me any mind."

"How long is it going to take to drain the lake?"

"Not long enough to suit me. I've had a time of it keeping kids off the ice." Jake pointed to the signs around the edge of the lake. Although he couldn't read them from here, he knew what they said: *Dangar! Thin Eyese!* Horace hired Debbie, a local eccentric who might or might not be D.B.Cooper, to make the signs on the cheap. But Horace forgot to check whether Debbie would try to spell things right this time, or if he would maintain his cover as an illiterate, crazy hillbilly. *No wonder D.B. Cooper got away from the law,* Jake thought.

"It'll be May before the water is low enough to see the foundations of the old resort and town," Jake said.

Dr. Dave tucked his hands under his arms to get warm. "Think you'll have more trouble than usual with tourists this year?"

4

Jake shrugged. "Who knows? The spring before you moved to town, someone tried to get salvage rights to the lake so he could dive down and poke around the old *Gold Standard.*"

"What happened?"

"Fort Smith blocked the application," Jake said. "Folks don't like to think some diver has been swimming around in their drinking water. They almost arrested Jimmy Fisher once when we caught him snorkeling off the reservoir tower. He swore he saw a flathead catfish the size of a VW bus, but that's just another General Custer tale."

"General Custer?" Dr. Dave's eyebrows drew together like knitting needles.

Jake laughed. "You mean there's a local legend you haven't heard yet?"

"Many, I'm sure," Dr. Dave said. "I haven't lived here that long.

Jake tapped his fingers on the wheel of the valve. "So the story goes, just after the Great War a doughboy stayed at *The Gold Standard* to recover from shell shock. This soldier had seen action all over: including Asia. He had a little fish in a jar that he'd been carrying around for luck. They say he released the fish into the creek out by the hotel. If you believe Horace and Jimbo, that fish survived and grew until it was the size of a school bus.

"I know goldfish live a long time, but that fish would be a century old!" Dr. Dave scratched his head.

Jake shrugged. "Horace and Jimbo have been after *him* for years. They've always said the reason there aren't any fish in Lake Tranquility is General Custer eats them all. Guess we'll know in a few months if he even exists," Jake said. "Unless the Big Bird ate him."

"Urban legend versus urban legend. That sounds like a wrestling match on pay per view," Dr. Dave said. "If General Custer did exist, you and Rachel would have to get a big stock tank and coordinate a rescue operation."

"What's this *me and Rachel* business?" Jake put his hands on his hips.

Dr. Dave pinned him with a stare. "You really think you could get out of a giant catfish rescue operation when you married a vet who talks to animals?"

Jake pursed his lips. "Good point. I think I'll ask the Fish and Game Department whether they have one, just in case. They've helped her in the past."

"Horace said there are some archaeology students coming down here to poke around," Dr. Dave said. "Maybe they'll help keep troublemakers away just by being here."

Jake leaned against the outflow valve. "I hope so. The old resort's name is the kind of thing that attracts treasure seekers. Nothin' but trouble. What was Rachel's great-granddaddy thinking naming his resort *The Gold Standard?*"

"You mean my great-granddaddy named *Coin*? I can't imagine." Rachel said as she waddled up. She wore a light jacket with the hood down. Her ferret Duke rode in the hood, while Lelani wrapped around her neck like a furry scarf.

Jake turned and opened his arms to her. Rachel bumped her pregnant belly against him, then turned sideways to hug him. "Why aren't you dressed warmer?" He asked.

She faked a punch at his arm and smiled. "The baby is like a little furnace."

"I heard you had trouble with Scott Walters?" Jake asked.

Rachel stroked Lelani's back. "Not really." She looked at Dr. Dave.

"Since you asked, *The Gold Standard* sounds less foreign than the *Hotel des Poitiers.*" Rachel pointed to the restored hotel overlooking the reservoir.

"That reminds me," Jake scratched his nose. "Remember the guy from the History Channel?"

Rachel crossed her arms. "Michael Moder. The one with the traveling TV crew you arrested because you thought he murdered all those people. What about him?"

"He wants to do a documentary on *The Gold Standard,*" Jake said.

"Why?" Dr. Dave asked. "I thought they specialized in documentaries on haunted places."

Jake scratched the back of his head, pushing his uniform hat up over his eyebrows in the process. "When I talked to him on the phone, he was going on about the romance of *The Gold Standard* bein' a lost city."

"A couple of concrete foundations and an amphitheater?" Rachel held her hands out, palms up.

"It's just another form of gold fever, Darlin'," Jake said. "He's done got permission from the Corps of Engineers and the City of Fort Smith to film the old resort. He wanted to know if you had any *Gold Standard* memorabilia he could use."

Rachel made a pushing motion with her hands. "Momma donated it all to the Tranquility Historical Society so she could get it out of the attic when she moved. Good thing, too. Otherwise Scott would be harassing her as well."

"Mr. Moder said he also wants to interview you, since you're one of the last descendants of the Coin family."

"Me?" She froze. "On TV? Nu-huh!"

Jake grinned. "You don't have to do anything you don't want to do, Darlin'."

She waved her hands in front of her face as if she hadn't heard him. "All my baby weight went straight into my face."

"I think you're gorgeous," Jake said.

Rachel glared at him. "You think I should do it, don't you?"

"Maybe you shouldn't." Jake grinned. "You might get discovered by some Hollywood-type. Then where would I be?"

She put her hands on her hips. "Now you're making fun of me."

"It *could* happen. An agent might think you would be a good host for Animal Planet."

"You're the one with the lucky streak, not me," Rachel said.

"He could put you behind a shade. Like you're going into witness protection or something."

"It's *Unsolved Mysteries* where they do that, Honey," Rachel said.

"Yes, dear," Jake replied.

"Speaking of TV," Dr. Dave pointed down the path they'd just walked up. "Here comes Horace and the news people." A yellow school bus with the words "Fort Smith Public School District" printed on the side pulled up. Horace led several city officials from the bigger city to the south, reporters and photographers out of the bus.

Jake separated the reporters from the city officials based on their dress. City officials wore American flag pins. The reporters looked like interviewees for a job with *GQ,* their suits more tailored than those worn by the city officials. The photographers in their collared t-shirts and cargo pants seemed like fraternity brothers on game day. Their bulky equipment was the single—and expensive—sign that they weren't here in a futile quest for a kegger.

A small SUV pulled up behind the bus. A wide-eyed, disheveled man tumbled from the driver's seat. He pulled several rolled up paper maps from his backseat, tucked them under his arm and then shoved his way through officials and reporters.

Rachel groaned. "Great! Scott."

"And you didn't want *me* to cause a scene." Jake shifted behind the control valve, using it as a shield between him and the media. He settled his hands on the wheel to wait for Horace's signal.

"I should take care of him now before he becomes a bigger pest." Rachel rolled her eyes as she waddled away. She met Scott before he reached the crowd and pulled him to the side to speak with him without interrupting the ceremony. Jake kept one eye on them, but Rachel seemed to appease Scott even as she propelled him back to his vehicle.

Horace and the officials from the Corps of Engineers and the City of Fort Smith lined up like ducks along the top of the dam. As the television crew set up, Horace twiddled his thumbs and shifted from one foot to another. Then he let out a nervous laugh.

Oh no. Jake thought. *He's going to say something stupid. On TV no less.*

"I hope you all enjoyed the dam press conference today," Horace said. "I trust we've answered all of your dam questions about the dam repairs. Now, let's get on with the dam ceremony."

"About dam time." Jake muttered, putting his weight behind the wheel to turn it. The rusty machinery groaned, but inched around. Water that trickled through a hole in the bottom of the embankment became a pounding, followed by a roar as it shot through the opening.

Jake heard a long creak followed by an ominous crack as the ice broke under its own weight.

Chapter 3: Two Weeks Ago

A relentless pounding noise pulled David from a dreamless sleep. He lifted his head—the pain in his neck reminded him of nights as an intern at Baptist-Hospital Memphis. Back when sleep meant leaning against a locker for five minutes.

He sat up in confusion. He felt...sticky.

His shirt and slacks oozed slime. When he moved, they made a sucking sound against the naugahyde sofa.

No loss there. I can just hose it off, he thought. With a groan, he stumbled to his feet. Every muscle in his body screamed in agony. *What happened to me last night?*

Like a drunkard with a bad hangover, he recalled flashes of being called down to Rachel's Vet clinic to help with a rough delivery.

I'm glad I'm not one of her patients. She's got the bedside manner of a drill instructor. He groaned. *I can't believe I birthed a calf. I had my arms in the back end of an actual cow.* He would have buried his face in his hands, except for the cow slime.

The pounding started again at his front door. He shambled, duck feet and bandy-legged to the entrance and tried to grasp the knob in the bend of his elbow to turn it. The lock rattled, but failed to budge.

"Dr. Dave?" Average Jones, David's maybe-girlfriend, called out. "Are you home?"

"Just a second!" David's voice sounded rusty from lack of use. He scissored the knob between his two wrists for a second try. When they slipped off, he kicked the door in frustration.

"What's wrong?" Average asked.

David held up his slime-covered hands in frustration. "I can't get the door open!"

"Why don't I just use the key under the mat?"

"I have a key under the door mat?" David asked in confusion.

Average stuck her head in the door. Her eyes traveled up and down his rangy frame. Her smile faltered, before growing even wider.

"Mrs. Paulson called the diner this morning. She said you would need a ride to work. At least, I think that's what she said. I can never tell when she has her precognition turned on and starts holding the conversation backwards."

David grunted. To think, he once believed having a psychic secretary would make his life easier. "She might have warned me about Rachel and the cow yesterday. I could've changed into...Fishing waders or something."

"You would have just hidden under your bed and pretended you weren't home." Average said.

David scoffed. Sometimes he hated having a maybe-girlfriend who could read his emotions. But that's what he got for dating an empath. "I can't wait for Rachel to have her kid. Then she can go back to doing all the disgusting physical jobs in her practice and leave me alone."

Average made to cross the threshold, but pulled up short at the last second. She frowned at his slimy clothing. Then she made a shooing motion.

David stepped back to let her pass.

"First time you ever pulled a calf?" she asked.

"Do I have to answer that?" He plucked at his shirt with his thumb and forefinger. "Is there anything that will clean cow slime out of clothes? These were custom-tailored."

Average patted the top of his head - the one dry spot on his body. "I'll take them back with me to the Dine-O-Mat," she said. "I can wash them between the breakfast and lunch rush." She hummed under her breath—as she did whenever she used her empathy gift to sooth him. "Why don't you shower? I'll find some glass cleaner and fix your couch."

David's tense muscles loosened. Some mornings Average worked better than a cup of coffee. "You're an angel," he said.

As Average headed for the Kitchen, he practically skipped down the hall toward the shower. Then, another knock sounded at the door. David stared at the bathroom in longing before going to answer it again.

This time it opened on the first try and his blood ran cold at the sight of the tall, statuesque blonde standing on his front step. In that moment, all of Average's good work unraveled.

Jody.

"Hello, David." As she sauntered past him into his living room, the cloying smell of her perfume invaded his senses, calling up hundreds of unpleasant memories. She studied his slimy clothes, the sticky naguahide furniture and the dilapidated state of the city-owned house. Then she gave him a knowing look. "How have you been?"

"Jody?" David spluttered. He'd fantasized about this moment thousands of times. Each time he appeared suave and debonair and countered her every comment with a sneer and a scathing quip. But never once while covered with slime, standing in run-down government housing.

He rubbed his eyes with the backs of his wrists. Surely this was some kind of stress-induced, post-natal, bovine break-from-reality.

Jody smiled at David's confusion. Just like when she'd thrown her infidelity in his face. "Who else would come to visit you?"

"Not you." David half-expected a TV crew to burst through the door. This was too much like the set up to a bad Japanese game show. Or maybe a Spanish tellenovella. Here was his ex-fiancée, looking great and smug while he looked like an escapee from an off-off-off-really-off Broadway production of *Les Misérables.* "What are you doing here?"

"I thought I would surprise you," she said. "I was in the neighborhood."

"Tranquility isn't in anyone's neighborhood," David said. "Even back in Memphis slumming it for you meant hanging out at the Peabody." He wished the earth would just open up and swallow her whole. Maybe with flames and lava.

A crack like rumbling thunder echoed down from above like answer to his silent prayer. The rumble rolled into an ominous creak as the ceiling split open like an egg.

Then the roof fell in.

David bent to avoid the rain of plaster, insulation and wood splinters, coughed and pulled the neckline of his shirt above his nose and mouth. He waved at the air in a futile effort to clear the dust.

As the plaster and noise settled, he squinted at the pile of debris. Jody's expensive Italian shoes poked from beneath the rubble like Ruby slippers on the feet of the Wicked Witch of the East—an apt description, come to think of it.

The corners of David's mouth pulled back in a wide grin. He turned his face toward the hole in the ceiling, and the heavens beyond.

"Thank You," he said to whatever higher power was listening.

As Dr. Dave opened the door, a tiny blonde bounced through the entrance and barely stopped from throwing herself around his mucous-covered body. She reminded Average of Marilyn Monroe in *Gentlemen Prefer Blondes*.

"Hi, David?" she said.

Was this odd girl someone from the past Dr. Dave never talked about? With burning curiosity Average opened her empathic shields so she could read the emotions they were sending.

She drew back at the disconnect between what she felt from the two of them and what her eyes told her. The girl fountained over with child-like buoyant happiness and innocent obliviousness. But from Dr. Dave came blind, murderous rage. Average's hand flew to her mouth.

He stared at the strange girl as if he didn't see her.

The girl prattled on, waving her hands in the air like a symphony conductor. "I'm studying at the university in Fayetteville now? Can you believe it? Me? In college? Mother used to say girls only need college to find a husband? Now I scandalized her? I mean, me? An archaeology student? Just like Laura Croft? I even have a cute pair of boots?" She stuck one foot out and wiggled it to show him.

"And when I heard about the dig here? In the town you moved to? I just had to sign up? I mean, can you believe it?"

Average wrinkled her forehead in confusion. The little blonde seemed harmless, like a pet bunny. Why the murderous rage from Dr. Dave?

Maybe the way she talks sets his teeth on edge, she thought. *I've never heard anyone make a question out of every statement.*

His abrupt, savage joy interrupted her musing. She scratched her head in confusion and then touched his shoulder. "Dr. Dave?"

He shook himself as if shaking off a dream-like state. His disappointment covered Average like a wet blanket—cold and heavy.

The girl broke out of her self-absorbed ramble long enough to realize she'd lost their attention. Her annoyance felt like prickles along Average's arms and left a taste like sour lime candy in the back of her mouth.

"Who're you?" She put her hands on her hips. Her nose twitched like a bunny's.

Average tucked her hands behind her back and rocked on her heels. "I was about to ask you the same thing."

They both turned to Dr. Dave for introductions. But he was studying his shoes. With a mental groan, Average stuck out her hand to shake. "Average Jones."

The girl tapped her foot, expecting more information. Average scanned the other girl's emotions while at the same time giving her a visual once-over. Her clothes didn't come from the local mall. She was no doubt status-conscious and curious about where Average ranked in the local social pecking order.

"My father's the mayor of Tranquility," she explained.

Just then Dr. Dave snapped out of his stupor. "Av, this is Jody. She's my ex. Jody, Average is my girlfriend." The words spilled out of his mouth.

What? Average whipped her head around. Sure, they dated casually. But that's as far as she intended to let it get until he dealt with his baggage. She didn't want to "fix" Dr. Dave's emotional train wrecks 24/7. Not her circus, not her monkeys.

But it looks like she'd just been handed a top hat and red coat, because a confusing goulash of dread, hope and contrition boiled inside the Doc. And Jody looked like she'd just lost her favorite toy.

Average squashed the urge to huff in annoyance. *It's like being in high school all over again. If I have to do this a second time, I should at least get a good sound track and some TV teen drama eye candy like Sebastian Stan.*

Jody's eyes grew as round as dinner plates as she looked from Average to the stains on David's clothing. "David?" she clamped her hands over her mouth and continued to talk around them. "You should lock your door when you and your girlfriend are being kinky?"

Dr. Dave flushed red to the tips of his ears. "Jeez, Jody! Clearly you still haven't developed a filter between your brain and your mouth."

"You used to like that I said what I thought?" Jody looked like a kicked puppy. "You said I was refreshingly honest?"

"Like a swim in ice water," he muttered.

Average bit her lip, unsure whether to pat Jody on the head or laugh. Instead she patted Dr. Dave's shoulder. The impact made a dull, squishing sound. "Maybe you two can catch up later. Doc was about to jump in the shower."

"Oh? Okay?" Jody brightened. "I've got to get back to my team anyway? We're going to go through the pictures of the old town under the lake? Maybe I'll see you at the restaurant later?"

"Maybe," Dr. Dave muttered without enthusiasm.

"Great? Bye, David?" she pounced closer to him and bent into an L shape to kiss his cheek without touching his disgusting clothes. Giggling, she ran out the door.

"*That's* your ex?" Average asked. Acute embarrassment rolled off of Dr. Dave.

"What?" He crossed his arms.

"I just expected someone more sinister."

"Butter wouldn't melt in her mouth," Dr. Dave said. "Don't let the bubble-brained bleach blond exterior fool you. She's so evil plastic plants wilt when she walks by."

"How did you wind up engaged to her?"

Dr. Dave ran his hands through his hair, accidentally slicking it back. "I didn't see the real her for years. She's good at hiding it. That's why doctors didn't smother her as an infant. I'm pretty sure at one point she had siblings but she must have cannibalized them when she was young."

"Dr. Dave," Average sang out to calm him with her empathy. She felt his distress ease a little.

"I'm being irrational, aren't I?" His shoulders slumped.

"Little bit." Average held her finger and thumb an inch apart.

Dr. Dave breathed in and held it for a second before letting it out as a drawn-out sigh. "I met Jody at a party for the hospital staff where I interned. Her dad's one of the members of the hospital board, and her mother organized the Memphis Ladies Auxiliary. Muffy and Duffy Alexander."

"Their names are Muffy and Duffy?" Average tilted her head sideways.

"Yes they are, *Average*."

"Point taken," Average muttered.

"Jody seemed fun. She had connections I didn't. I guess that made us a power couple. Except I wasn't holding up my end of the bargain. According to Jody, I would bring home the bacon and she would fry it up in the pan."

"I think that's a line from an old song," Average said.

"That figures." Dr. Dave rolled his eyes. "She's pretty and she ran with the right crowd. I used to be as deep as a kiddie pool. You know what she said when I found out she was cheating?"

"What?"

"Lighten up, David?" Dr. Dave parroted Jody's habit of making every statement both a question and an exclamation. "Everyone has open relationships these days?"

"If it's not a big deal, why couldn't she have told you before she got caught?" Average wondered.

"That's what I asked her."

"That's messed up," Average said.

"She claimed to have no idea she hurt me. Couldn't see what the big deal was. If she hadn't been so "clueless," I might have stayed in Memphis. I still would have broken our engagement, but I could have just changed hospitals. But most of the people I knew called me crazy for letting *a little thing* like her infidelity get in the way of our picture-perfect future. After that, I knew I couldn't stay."

"I feel sorry for her," Average said.

Dr. Dave scoffed.

"It sounds like she grew up in a family of takers. It's all she knows. And from the sound of it, your breaking up with her rocked her world."

"I doubt it."Dr. Dave scoffed. "Jody glides through life like Glenda the Good Witch in her own little bubble."

"She said she's in college and it upset her mother."

"Her mother only gets upset when she runs out of valium."

Average reached for him, then turned it into an awkward pat on the back of his neck: the second least messy point on his body. "I'll call dad and have him brew up a fresh pot of coffee just for you."

"Sounds wonderful," Dr. Dave said. He paused on his way to the bathroom. "I shouldn't wonder if this day can get any worse. It always does. Maybe I'm developing special powers like everyone here: powers of pessimism."

"You. Shower." Average pointed down the hallway.

"Yes, Ma'am," Dr. Dave said.

Alice sat at the kitchen table with her hands folded. She stared up at the ceiling, taking a sip from a cup of hot tea every once in a while.

"Well?" She asked.

"I'm sorry, Alice," Mabel's ghost said, whisper-quiet in her ear. "Winn has his soap recipe memorized. And I can't learn by watching him make it."

"Why not?" Alice sipped her tea again.

"There's something in the soap fumes. I can't go near them."

Alice hummed in thought. *It whitens and it repels ghosts. It must have a high sodium content.*

"Can we still play along with the game shows together? I've got nothing else to do." Mabel sounded hopeful.

Alice wanted to scold her departed friend for not making more of an effort to have a social un-life with other spirits. When *she* died, the grass might grow over her grave but she wouldn't let it grow under her spectral feet.

Until then, she was stuck having slumber parties for the undead. She buried her head in her hands. Why couldn't she find uses for this gift, like Whoopi Goldberg or Hailey Jo Osment did in those movies? Why couldn't she help people complete unfinished business and move into the light? She wondered if Sarah Winchester went crazy for the same reasons.

"Of course we can, Mabel." She rubbed her eyes. "Wheel of Fortune is on tonight."

Just then Alice felt her daughter Anna's presence enter the room.

"Aren't you dating Elvis and haunting Graceland?" Alice made a sour face.

"You never visit," Anna said.

"Memphis is all the way across Arkansas from here," Alice said. "And it's not like Priscilla or Lisa Marie will let me stay in the Jungle Room rent-free. So the most I can afford is once or twice a year. You want me to visit more often, haunt someplace local."

"The Jungle Room isn't a bedroom."

"So?"

"Dad asked me to check on you." Anna continued as if she hadn't heard Alice.

"Your father could speak to me himself if he would stop being such a stubborn horse's--"

"Mother!"

"At least you're not here to stalk Jake."

"Why would I stalk Jake? He has Rachel now. Why are you and Winn feuding?"

"He's holding my soap supply hostage so Jake will let him out of a few fines."

Anna snorted. "I also heard you have *someone* spying on Winn."

Mabel let out a small yelp and Alice heard the sound of fleeing feet. She wondered how ghosts could make running sounds. Oh well, at least she was off the hook for watching *Wheel of Fortune* with Mabel tonight.

"Are we trying to catch him in the act of making his bootleg whisky?" Anna asked in a singsong voice.

"His soap recipe, actually," Alice said. "If he won't sell me his soap, I'll make my own. That'll show him!"

"You're acting like you're at war with him," Anna said.

"It's the principle of the thing," Alice snapped.

Chapter 4

Jake hurried down the stairs as incessant pounding rattled the front door of the house. He glanced back up to see Rachel roll her eyes and Tommy copy the maneuver.

"Oh gee, it's spring, and classes have got to be over. I wonder who that could be?" Sarcasm dripped from Rachel's words. She put a finger to her chin in mock wonder. "Is it possibly Scott Walters, maybe?"

Tommy hopped from one foot to the other. "Are you going to shoot him this time, Dad? I can go get Rachel's tranquilizer gun!"

"No one's shooting anyone," Jake said. "And watch the attitude, young man. Just because Rachel can't control herself doesn't mean I'll excuse your smart mouth." He turned away. In the mirror on the landing he could see Rachel and Tommy exchange a fist-bump. "You get out of sight," he told Rachel. "If it is Scott, I'll get rid of him."

"Try to make this quick!" Rachel called after him. "Alice is expecting Tommy soon and I have to meet Mr. Moder at the diner."

Just as Rachel guessed, Scott Walters stood on the porch, fist raised to knock again when Jake opened the door.

Jake considered taking Tommy up on the offer of the tranq gun for a moment. Instead, he stepped onto the porch and closed the door behind him. Then he assessed Scott's appearance for threat level.

The kid had red-rimmed, puffy eyes like he'd been through several caffeine-fueled sleepless nights. He wore a loose button down shirt that made him seem smaller and carried a sheaf of papers under his arm.

At least he smelled like he'd bathed, so he wasn't quite as crazed as last winter when he'd shown up uninvited to Horace's press conference. If Jake had to guess, as soon as finals ended, Scott went straight from studying history to studying old newspapers and maps relating to *The Gold Standard* and the Coin treasure.

"Jake!" Scott clasped his left elbow with his right hand behind his back. "I didn't expect to see you. Your patrol car isn't in your garage."

"It's parked up at the lake to discourage gawkers," Jake said. "You finished your classes for the semester?"

Scott craned his neck to peer over Jake's shoulder and through the glass windows in the front door. "Yeah. I passed, so I can remain a professional student for another semester. Is Mrs. Rachel in?"

Gripping Scott's shoulder, Jake steered him down the front steps. "I know you're excited about the lake draining and Old Man Coin's treasure. But what did we talk about last year?"

Scott stuck his lower lip out. "I'm supposed to set up an appointment to talk to Mrs. Rachel through the Historical Society?"

"Do you remember why?" Jake asked.

"Because Mrs. Rachel can't drop everything to see my research whenever I show up? But it's important, Jake! I think there are subterranean caves under the lake! Old Mr. Coin must have sealed them off, but the seals are failing! Why else would the water level drop so fast?"

Jake dragged his hand down his face. "Scott, the geologists aren't concerned about the lake levels."

"I bet you *that* won't last." Scott slumped and crossed his arms.

"Now listen, Scott. Rachel has a baby on the way and a clinic to run. Last time you barged in unannounced, you scared off her clients. It's fine to talk to her. Just respect her boundaries. If you don't, we'll file a restraining order."

Scott chewed on his lip for a while, then nodded. "Okay, Jake. I'll head over to the Historical Society when they open and set up an appointment."

"Good," Jake said. "And stay away from the lake. It's not safe. Some of the terrain is boggy like quicksand right now. If you want to poke around, there's an archaeology group coming down from the University to study the old town. Volunteer to help them out."

The kid flashed him a thumbs-up. "Thanks for the tip." Then he ran for his SUV, juggling the papers as he went.

Back in the house Jake found Tommy, nose pressed against a window, watching Scott leave. "Why not just tranq him and be done with it?"

Jake shook his head. "What did I tell you?"

Tommy sighed. "Just because Rachel does it, don't mean it's okay."

"That's right." Jake laughed.

The smell of spring always clung to the Tranquility Dine-O-Mat, thanks to the coin-operated laundromat half of the business. But another smell attracted David this morning: dark, rich Columbian roast.

His world narrowed to the near-empty pot Horace Jones held in his hands.

"My coffee," he said.

Average touched his shoulder. "Dad'll have another pot brewed up in a jiffy."

David ignored her. He cut across the diner to the counter where Jake held out a cup for a refill, pushing everything out of his way. David stared at the cup as Horace poured the dregs into it. He licked his parched lips and fought to swallow.

Jake grinned and handed the cup to David. "I think you need this more than I do, Dr. Dave."

David took the drink and cradled it as if holding Holy Communion. He raised it to his lips with both hands. It slid over his tongue with the consistency of motor oil and tasted like the bottom of an ash tray.

It was the best coffee David ever tasted in his life.

"Thirsty?" Jake laughed.

"Can I get this in an I.V. drip?" David sat the empty cup down and turned to survey the chaos he had left in his wake. Debbie wore an overturned bowl of cereal on his lap and an angry scowl on his face. He flipped the bird in David's direction. Average stood next to him, crooning in soothing tones while mopping at his shirt with a paper napkin. In a corner booth, Rachel looked on in amusement.

"Sorry. Medical emergency?" David held up his empty mug.

"What's the rush, Dr. Dave?" Horace topped off Jake's cup from a fresh pot and then refilled David's.

"I pulled a cow last night for Rachel." He shuddered. "They didn't cover *that* in school."

Horace let out a low whistle. "You should have come by last night. I could have fixed you up with some of Winn's special brew."

Jake set his cup down. "I'm not hearing the mayor say he serves illegal booze in a dry county. I know nothing."

"Not his alcohol, Jake! I meant his lye soap!"

"That's different," Jake said. "You should get some, if you can. Winn uses his mother's secret recipe. Back before his wife passed away, he wouldn't let her help make it so she couldn't find out the secret. God rest her soul."

Horace leaned over to David's ear and cupped his hands to whisper. "He uses it to scrub out his still."

"It'll scare the germs right off of you." Jake talked over Horace.

"I'm not sure I want to use anything harsh enough that germs run in fear from it," David said. "But Average helped me clean up the house. She said she would do the same for my clothes."

"If you manage to get any of Winn's soap, don't tell Alice," Jake added. "Not if you want to keep it. She swears it's all she can use for cleaning her house. But last time she wanted a batch from Winn, he wouldn't sell her any."

"Why not?" David hadn't heard about any problems between the mother of Jake's late wife and Tranquility's resident bootlegger.

"He wants Jake to drop a couple of fines," Horace said.

"I can't!" Jake stared down into his coffee cup with a frown. "Not even for my mother-in-law. Rachel's taking lye soap in partial trade for services at the clinic and giving it to Alice."

David scratched his head.

"Winn didn't try to do this to Rachel, because he needs her to take care of his sick critters, Jake said. "She could turn them against him."

"But can't Rachel just withhold services on Alice's behalf until Winn promises to sell his goods to her again?" David asked.

"Would you withhold services from one of your patients?" Jake asked.

"Point," David said.

"I hope Alice and Winn will work this out without dragging the whole city into it."

"Winn doesn't really have a beef with Alice at all. Can't you just cancel the fines?" David turned to Horace. "You're the mayor. Don't you have the authority?"

Horace made a choking sound and clutched at his heart.

"Sorry," David said. "Forgot who I was talking to. This is worse than a tellenovella. All we're missing is some guy named Carlos."

Sarah, the manager of the *Hotel des Portiers,* walked in dressed in her Gibson-girl dress uniform and hairstyle. Jake nodded his greetings as she sat down and motioned for a cup of coffee. She had a haggard appearance, with wisps of hair escaping her upswept style and dark circles under her face.

"Hello, Sarah," David said.

A tired smile crossed her face. "Good morning."

"Are you alright?" Jake asked.

"Just burning the midnight oil," she said. "With the lake going away, the tourists are too. I'm scrambling to fill the vacancy with dam repairmen."

Jake leaned in toward her. "I hope the hotel isn't in trouble," He whispered.

Sarah threw a guarded look over her shoulder. "Not at all," she mouthed. Louder, she said: "I've filled enough vacancies to cover the bills and satisfy our investors. The workers should finish during the slow season, and by next year the tourists will come back. It'll be lean times, but we'll get through."

"Good to hear," Jake said.

A hand slipped around David's shoulder and rubbed at his chest. "Hello, David."

David's fist clenched around his mug handle. "What do you want, Jody?"

"I thought we decided to meet for coffee." Jody strutted around him and stood with her hip cocked against the counter. Her mannerisms seemed off, like an alien in a Jody suit. "I've toured your little town. It's very quaint. Very different from home."

"Great! Maybe you should go back there."

"I heard from your mother that this town is dripping with treasure." She pulled his cup of coffee from his hands, drank his last sip and delivered a slow, challenging wink over the rim of the mug. When she put it down, she wore a smirk of triumph. "You would never know it from the look of this place, though."

A look of alarm crossed her face. She held a well-manicured hand to her throat and made choking sounds. David held the mug up so he could see the bottom of it. He sniffed the rim. Then he looked around the room. No one else noticed Jody's signs of distress. It was as if she were invisible. Then she collapsed to the floor and lay still.

"Hi David?"

Average watched as Jody bounced through the door of the restaurant. Judging by the denim coveralls and grubby sneakers she now wore, she'd already been down to the lake to poke around. Her perky blonde ponytails had cute little streaks of dirt in them and a smudge of mud crossed her forehead.

Jody collided with Dr. Dave, knocking over his mug and pulling him into a bear hug. Dr. Dave's eyes glazed over and the rage Average sensed earlier came rushing back. She turned to the table where Mr. Hunley sat, waiting for her to take his order.

"Would you excuse me for a minute, Mr. Hunley? I think Dr. Dave may need me."

Mr. Hunley craned his neck so he could see Jody over Average's shoulder. "Who is the escapee from Romper Room?"

"Dr. Dave's friend from Memphis." Average kicked herself as the interest of the other diners perk up. She hadn't meant to, but she'd just added fuel to the Tranquility rumor mill.

Mr. Hunley squinted at Dr. Dave. "Take your time," he said.

Jake waved a hand in front of Dr. Dave's face. The Doc remained in a trancelike state. Average handed her order pad to her dad and then prodded Dr. Dave's shoulder. "Are you alright?"

Dr. Dave jumped. As he startled, Jody let go of him and backed away. Average felt the other girl's annoyance at losing everyone's attention again.

He shook himself. "What happened?"

"You spaced out for a second," Jake said. "Did you get enough sleep last night?"

"I got enough to get by." Dr. Dave's gaze sidled over to Jody. He radiated disappointment.

Average worried her lip. As soon as she got away from the diner, she would corner Dr. Dave and find out why he kept zoning out. In the meantime, she could make up for Dr. Dave's rudeness by being nice to Jody. "Have you been up to the lake?"

"Lake?" Jody looked confused. Average pointed to Jody's forehead. "Because of the dirt."

"Oh? No, I just unloaded our soil strainers?"

"She talks strange," Horace whispered behind his hand to Jake.

"Like the little pink pony in the cartoon I watch with Tommy." Jake nodded.

Horace gave Jake a funny look. "What kind of cartoons are you watching?"

"Don't judge until you see it," Jake said.

Dr. Dave glared at them to shut them up. "Why're you here again?" He asked Jody. Although his words radiated hostility, Jody seemed oblivious.

"I told you, because of the dig?" she said.

"No." Dr. Dave slapped his face into his palm. He held it for a minute as if searching for reserves of patience. "I *mean*: how did you end up studying archeology? Last time I saw you, you wouldn't walk across a parking lot because you had sandals and the dirt might ruin your pedicure."

She laughed. "Wasn't that silly of me?" She nodded and Average found herself nodding along. Jody tucked her hands into her pockets in a self-depreciating way. "When you left me—It got me thinking, you know? No one ever left me before? I mean? It couldn't be my fault? I mean? Me? Daddy always said I was perfect? But then I took stock of my life and I think maybe I was just a teeny tiny smidge...Not so perfect? I mean? Did I want the life my parents have? To be a trophy wife?

Spend my time on the treadmill? Shopping trips to Dallas? Planning the Junior League Holiday Bazaar? Traded in on a younger model by 45? Bitter? Living on alimony? Alcoholic? Just like my mother? Can you imagine? I thought maybe you had the right idea? If you could reinvent yourself, why couldn't I?"

"So you decided to go for a PhD?" Dr. Dave asked.

"It seems strange, but I think history's my calling? At least until I can get at my trust fund?"

Dr. Dave buried his face in his hands. "I see you've thought this through."

She grinned. "I almost joined the Peace Corps to help orphans in Africa? But I could get all kinds of horrible diseases there? And here I can still get my hands dirty? Just like someone respectable? See?" She held out her dirt smeared hands for him to see. Despite the grime, she still had a perfect manicure.

"Oh? And best of all? I met Marco?" She bounced in place and squealed.

"Who is Marco?" Horace asked.

She spun around and ran to the door. Then she stuck her head out and motioned into the parking lot. A tall guy with olive skin and dark hair joined her. He had a few lines around his face and gray at his temples. She took his hand and pulled him into the diner.

"Everyone? I'd like you to meet Marco Casari?" She held her hands out as if to say *tada!* "Marco? This is everyone?"

"Hello." Nervousness radiated off of Marco in waves.

"Hello." Average shook his hand. *New boyfriend meets the old boyfriend.* "Are you an archeology student, too?"

"Not...No." Marco let out a shaky laugh as he ran his hands through his hair. "I'm more of a professor. Professor Casari."

"Carlos. Marco. Close enough," Dr. Dave muttered. Average elbowed him in the ribs. "Welcome to Tranquility," he added in a flat tone. "I hope you find what you're searching for."

Marco and Jody traded looks. "We expect to," Marco said.

"While you're here, you should talk to Mr. Moder when he's done talking to Rachel," Jake pointed at a booth where Rachel sat alone cooing over her bald ferret.

Average tilted her head sideways. Moder. Why did that name sound familiar? Then it hit her. He headed the TV crew from *Ghost Chasers*. The ones filming at the haunted hotel last spring.

"He's making a documentary on *The Gold Standard* resort and the old town," Jake said. "He may want you for his documentary. At the very least you two should coordinate so you don't get in each other's way."

Marco jerked his head in a curt motion. Average felt his interest spike. "We'll talk to him before we start working."

"When will you do that?" Horace asked.

"We'll drive down from the college in Fayetteville until the lake drains," Marco said. Once we start excavating, we'll camp there to make sure no one messes with our work."

Average felt vague relief emanating from Jake. She bet he couldn't wait for someone else to take over lake security detail.

The moment Lady Elane entered the diner, she homed in on Rachel's pregnant belly like a baby-seeking missile, putting her hand on it before Rachel could have said "awkward stranger encounter." Rachel wondered how to extract herself from the situation. She motioned to Average for help, but the waitress shrugged in response.

Duke stuck his head out of Rachel's hood and made a dooking sound in excitement. *Treats? Does she have treats?*

When Lady Elaine failed to give him so much as a peanut butter flavored chip, the little ferret hissed. *No treats! Stupid hooman bean!*

Rachel patted his head as he retreated into the hood. She wished she could hide that easily.

"Boy or girl?" Lady Elane asked.

"Boy," Rachel said. She couldn't just say "Get your hands off of me" to one of Lord Valentine's friends. Not politely.

"Any morning sickness?"

"A little," Rachel hedged.

"One of my friends puked so much when she was pregnant, she wound up in the hospital."

Average waved to Rachel, then pointed at the door. Rachel turned and saw Michael Moder walk in. She stood in relief.

"'scuse me! I forgot! I have to iron my dog!" She hurried across the room.

"Hello?" Michael took a step back.

"Sorry, you know how people can get when you're pregnant," Rachel said, nodding her head towards Elaine.

He gave her a half-smile in understanding. "How big was the elephant she gave birth to, and did they need the Jaws of Life?

Rachel chuckled. Then noticed he didn't have a camera. She choked her laugher off as disappointment stabbed through her. She'd fixed her hair for this.

"I thought you wanted to film our interview?" She shifted Duke from her hood into the roomy front pocket of her jacket.

"Are you wearing eyeliner?" He asked. "You didn't wear makeup when you were planning your wedding."

"I wasn't on camera then!" She snapped. "With all this baby weight, my face is as big as a house, maybe it needed painting!"

"I'm sorry." He gave her a smile as weak as her mama's coffee. "I should have mentioned I wouldn't have a camera with me today. This is just a preliminary interview so I can find out more about the old resort. When the lake drains, we'll film you on location."

"Oh." Rachel lowered her head, somewhat mollified.

Michael produced a spiral notebook from his satchel and paged through it. "Thanks for directing us to the Historical Society. We're using their pictures to create a computer reconstruction of the old town."

"I can't wait to see it!" Rachel said as she led him back to her booth.

He pulled out a pen and held it poised over a page to take notes. "What do you think about the rumors there is treasure buried somewhere under *The Gold Standard*?"

"If there was one, do you think Great-Granddaddy would have gone bankrupt and lost *The Gold Standard*?"

"You mean the government foreclosed on the property?" Michael looked up. "Every record I have said they seized it through eminent domain."

"Some friends in high places kept things hushed up out of respect for him," Rachel said. "Grandma used to say Great-

Grandaddy was embarrassed by what happened: a former candidate for governor, gone bankrupt. Imagine the scandal! But talking about it won't hurt now.

"With the number of treasure hunters who've plagued our family over the years, I wish Grampy'd been a bit more open about how little money he had."

"The rumors confused me." Michael studied his notes. "I found at least three contradicting stories about treasure. What is the fabled treasure supposed to be?"

Rachel laughed. "Just three? There are so many *lost treasure* stories in town, they get all mixed up sometimes. The one I hear most goes: Great-Granddaddy Coin found some treasure hid by the Spanish and buried it under his amphitheater. It's just a variation of another story about buried Spanish gold around here. There's also a story that Belle Starr gave him a cache of stolen loot for safekeeping."

"Who is she?" Michael's pen made a scratching sound as he wrote.

"She's a famous outlaw." Rachel pointed north. "She owned a farm a few miles from here in Winslow. Jake could tell you more. He's the expert on local history."

His fingers flew faster as he scribbled in his notebook. "Where do rumors say her loot came from?"

"Any number of places. Folks called her the bandit queen because she organized all the local cattle rustlers, bootleggers and horse thieves. Her brother rode with Quantrell's raiders. One rumor is that Cole Younger is the daddy of her daughter Pearl—who grew up to operate a brothel in Fort Smith."

"Cole Younger?"

"As in the James-Younger gang. Frank and Jessie James. But I don't think my great-grandpa would have associated with the likes of them. If it's speculation you want, there's a treasure hunter around here who could give you your money's worth. Scott Walters has heard all the rumors and he believes every single one."

Michael wrote down the name.

"If Great-Granddaddy Coin hid any kind of treasure, it would have been in the time capsule."

"I read about that." Michael flipped through pages of notes until he found a particular spot. He put his finger on the passage to mark it. "Convinced society would someday crumble, Hamish Coin collected blueprints from technology of the day and preserved it as a record to future civilizations."

"Mom told me they buried a time capsule somewhere on the property. Because we never found Great-Granddaddy Coin's records, no one knows where."

"If there is one, the archaeologists will find it," Michael said.

She picked up her mug and drank. "I think my great-granddaddy would like that."

His brow furrowed. "How so?"

"Great-Granddaddy Coin wanted to leave a record for future generations. Because of his quirks, he managed to catch your attention. Now with the lake draining, the University is putting him in the public record."

"Jake!" Jimmy Fisher ran through the doorway, his hands waving in the air. Jake half-stood. Jimmy stopped in front of him, panting. "There's something in the lake!"

"General Custer!" Horace whooped from the other side of the counter. "I knew it!"

Jimmy shook his head. "No giant fish. That's not what I saw."

"What, then?" Jake asked.

"There's a dead body out there!"

The restaurant fell silent.

Jake grabbed Jimmy's shoulders and forced the boy to look him in the eyes. "You're not making this up, are you Jimmy?"

Jimmy *could* have made it up, Rachel thought. That boy did strange things for attention.

"Jeez, you build one unsanctioned nuclear reactor and you're marked for life," Jimmy said.

"Jimmy." Jake shook his finger in warning.

Jimmy held up his hand as if swearing an oath. "I'm telling the truth!"

Jake met Rachel's gaze from across the room in a silent question. Would she like to go check things out with him? She nodded back.

"We'll have to continue this later, Michael. I think Jake and I are going to investigate."

"Right behind you." Michael shut his binder with a snap. The other patrons of the diner waved at Average for their checks. Horace shut down the grill, hung up his apron and pulled on his old fedora.

"We're going to have a lot of company," Rachel told Jake as she eased her rounded middle out of the booth.

Tracy S. Morris

Chapter 5

The body of Scott Walters lay on its back on top of some kind of stone post sticking out of the water. His head lolled and his arms and legs bent backward.

Jake made a face. "I hate this day already."

Rachel pulled at his arm. "That's…"

"Yep." He popped the P when he said it.

"He was just at our house."

"About an hour ago."

"I thought he was going over to the Historical Society?"

"Me too," Jake said.

"What is the body caught on?" Rachel asked in a whisper.

"No idea." Jake thought it looked like a brown Lincoln log or discolored Lego brick sitting on a mirror. But the body blocked his view from the muddy embankment of the lake's earthen dam.

A clatter behind them caused Jake to turn. The diner patrons, including Dr. Dave and Average, stopped short at the sight of the body. As if taking a step closer would somehow profane the dead. But Horace stumbled down the incline, sending a shower of pebbles rolling their way. The mayor caught the policeman's other arm to keep his balance when he reached them.

"Is that a chimney?" Horace doubled over, gasping for air. "I thought you said the Corps of Engineers knocked down everything from the old resort before the lake went through."

"What do you think, Darlin'?" Jake turned to face Rachel.

She scanned the lake, then puffed her cheeks out. "I don't know, Jake. Scott's the one person who knew more about the resort than me." She pointed at the body.

Jake squinted at the lake. "We'll get a better look when we retrieve the remains."

"You going for a swim, Jake?" Horace asked.

"I don't have to," Jake said. "The Police Department bought a John Boat last summer, remember? I can float out there and bring him back."

Horace turned white. "Er..."

Jake tapped his foot. "Let me guess. I'm not going to find it in the garage at City Hall parked next to the fire truck, am I?"

Horace scratched the back of his head and chuckled.

"You? Stealing city property?" Rachel scoffed. "Why am I not surprised?"

"Borrowed," Horace said. "I just borrowed it temporary-like."

"Then you won't complain when I requisition another one in a year or two when this one falls apart, will you?" Jake said.

"Now hold on Jake! Jimbo and I were performing a community service."

"You and the pharmacist?" Jake asked. "The only 'community service'," he made air quotes with his fingers, "that I can think of that involves you, Jimbo and a John Boat also involves a fishing pole and a six pack."

"Or maybe a stick of dynamite," Rachel added under her breath.

"With the lake level dropping this may be the best shot we have at General Custer," Horace said.

Rachel leaned forward in excitement, all annoyance forgotten. "Did you see him?"

"No such luck." Horace's head whipped around to the lake. "If that's a chimney, maybe he's hiding wherever it leads. Wouldn't that be something?"

"You ever see the movie Jaws?" Jake asked. "If this fish is as large as you think it is, it could eat you, Jimbo and the boat in one bite."

Horace scratched his chin. "You think so? Maybe he killed the fella out there on the lake. I guess we're going to need a bigger boat.

"Or you could just wait until the water drains," Jake said. "If there is a General Custer, he'll get stuck high and dry."

Horace whipped his hat off of his head and held it over his heart. "Perish the thought, Jake! A fish like General Custer should go down just like his namesake. In a blaze of glory."

Jake almost pointed out that the actual Custer was a jerk who died because he made the tactical blunder of attacking superior numbers. Instead he chewed the inside of his cheek and stared along the embankment of the lake. The folks from the diner and a few curious tourists clustered in groups behind the three of them to gawk at the macabre scene.

Jake cupped his hands in a megaphone around his mouth. "Folks? How about ya'll go about your business? There ain't nothing more to see here, so let's give the dead some respect."

The crowd spread out as if each person thought they could look like they were leaving while at the same time hanging around.

Jake spotted Billy and Emmitt, the two police academy washouts who worked as security guards at the hotel on the hill. His right eye twitched. "Oh look! Barney Fife and Gilligan!" He muttered.

Rachel hid a smile behind her hand. "Why don't you send them after the boat? That way you can stay here."

"If I do that, I have to talk to them." Jake groaned at the thought.

"Or you could get it yourself," Rachel said.

Jake calculated how long it would take for them to retrieve Emmet's truck, avoid Sarah so they didn't have to explain why they left their posts, go to Jimbo's pharmacy for the John Boat and return. He decided if he went himself, someone might try to swim out for a better look in his absence and drown or something. His rubbed his temples.

"Hey Billy? You and Emmet want to be deputized again?"

Billy made an expression like a confused bullfrog: mouth open, eyes bulging. He pointed to himself as if certain Jake meant someone else. Then he scrambled down the side of the hill with Emmet behind him. The two of them kicked up another micro-avalanche of rocks and dust which went tumbling into the lake.

"Yessir Jake!" Billy sketched off a salute. Jake barely kept himself from face palming in exasperation. He could hear Rachel laughing behind him.

"You can count on us! Who do you want to arrest? We always get our man! Just--"

"Please go get Emmet's truck." Jake cut across Billy's excited spiel. It was like watching a puppy wet on itself.

"We can run up to the hotel and get it right quick!" Billy danced from one foot to the other.

"Good! Yes. Fine. Take it down to the pharmacy. You'll find the city boat parked out back. Tell Jimbo you're getting it for me."

"If he don't want to give it to us, we can shoot him can't we?" Billy asked.

Alarm shot through Jake. "When did you start carrying guns?"

Billy looked as confused as a skunk spraying Old Spice. "We didn't. Sarah said we couldn't. But we've got tasers!"

"Leave the tasers back at the hotel," Jake said. "Don't tase anyone! Jimbo won't give you a lick of trouble. He'll want to lock up the pharmacy and come watch. Have him call Winn, while you're at it. He's the coroner, so we need him to declare the dead guy dead."

"Alright, Jake." Billy's shoulders sagged. "You sure you don't want us to carry our tasers? We could—"

"No!" Jake said. "No tasers and hurry!"

Emmet and Billy saluted again then stumbled and crawled their way back up the embankment.

"I'm going to regret that, ain't I?" He asked Rachel and Horace.

"At least they're willing to work without pay," Horace said. "That's the important part."

"Just so long as you're keeping things in perspective," Jake said.

By the time Billy and Emmet returned with Jimbo and Winn, it seemed like the other half of the town also turned up. To keep them back, he and Rachel set up a barrier with crime scene tape.

"As quick as the lake is draining, we won't even need a boat in a week."

Jimbo eased down the embankment to where they stood and squinted at the body. "Is that the big to-do?" The pharmacist asked. "I thought someone caught General Custer."

"No, but if that's the old resort then I bet it's where he's hiding," Horace said.

"Think so?" Jimbo rubbed at his chin. "How soon can we borrow back the John Boat?"

Horace watched Jake from the corner of his eye. "We should use Winn's pontoon boat. General Custer might be too big for the John Boat to handle."

"Good thinking," Jimbo said. "He'll bring some of his special brew for us to celebrate when we find The General."

Rachel threw her hands in the air, no longer pretending not to hear them. "If Winn brings his *special brew*, you won't catch anything. You'll be too drunk to fish."

"Ignore her," Jimbo said. "She's just defending Alice, anyway."

"Better tie yourself to the boat so you don't fall in." Rachel crossed her arms as she waddled down the lakeshore away from them.

Emmet pointed at the old boat ramp and tugged on Billy's sleeve. The cement ended about a dozen yards from the current lake level.

"Emmet's right," Billy said. "We can't back the boat down into the water."

Jake knocked on the side of the John Boat, a flat-bottomed, lightweight craft designed for skimming over shallow depths. "I think four of us can carry this thing," he said.

He pointed to the back of the craft, then to Emmet and Billy. "You two grab the aft."

"Aft?" Billy scratched his head.

"As in after. The back of the boat," Horace said.

Jake looked through the gathered crowd for someone both strong and competent enough to help. He spotted Dr. Dave. Perfect.

"Dr. Dave? Can you help me carry the front of the boat?" Jake asked.

Dr. Dave grabbed the edge of the boat. The four of them lifted the frame and squelched through the mud to the shore. Once there, they slipped the craft into the water with a tiny splash.

"Rachel, you and Dr. Dave want to come with me?"

"Why them?" Billy cut in. "Emmet and I are the ones you deputized!"

Jake rounded on Billy. "Unless one of you has a medical degree I don't know about, I don't need you anymore."

Billy stumbled across a rock and fell onto his rear.

Jake held his hand out to Rachel. Before she could reach him, Michael Moder waved him down.

"I hope you're not filming this," Jake said.

The documentary maker held up his hands in a show of surrender. "The censors would never allow it. But could you let me know what you find? This might catapult us into primetime!"

"Your concern is touching," Rachel said.

They got into the boat without Michael and Jake pushed off. Once they drifted far enough away from the bank, he put down the trolling motor. Rachel leaned forward, squinting. "It's a pipe of some kind!"

Dr. Dave craned to see around Rachel's shoulder. "There's something under the water!"

"Where?" Jake half-stood. The boat rocked, forcing all three of them to brace against the side. Rachel shot Jake a dirty look.

"Sorry!" Jake said.

Rachel pointed. "Whatever is underwater is near that pipe."

"Stay in your seat. I'll steer us there," Jake said. As they glided through the water, an algae-covered concrete platform took shape just under the surface.

"I think it's the top of the tower from the old resort," Rachel said.

"Great-Granddaddy Coin built the dining hall of *The Gold Standard* on the highest hill to make it the tallest building in town. When the bank ended up taller, he added a stone tower to one end of the hall," Rachel said. "If the tower is here, the bank's over there." She pointed to the center of the lake. "The rest of the old town used to fan out across the valley."

"Tallest? What about The *Hotel des Poitiers* up the hill?" Jake asked.

"It didn't count. The hotel wasn't in city limits," Rachel said. "One thing's for sure: Michael Moder's documentary just got a lot more interesting."

"It would be fascinating, if not for the body." Jake regarded Scott's remains. "We saw him alive a little over an hour ago."

"That makes time of death easy to determine," Dr. Dave said. "No bloating, so he wasn't in the water long. Move around to his head."

As they drew closer, Dr. Dave slipped on a pair of blue latex gloves. He touched Scott Walters's head and tilted it to the side. Then he slid open the body's jaw and peered into his mouth, followed by his nose. At last, he picked up one of the body's hands and studied it.

"Based on the foam in his mouth and nose, he was alive but unconscious when he went into the water," Dr. Dave said. "He's got abrasions on his elbow and a bruise on the side of his head. He might have fallen and hit his head."

Jake looked over Scott's clothes. The shoulder seemed muddy on the side where Scott's head was bruised. "He could have landed on his shoulder and then rolled into the water."

Dr. Dave hesitated. "Maybe."

Jake gave the Doc a sideways look. "You don't sound convinced."

Dr. Dave opened, then closed his mouth. "It's just the angle of this bruise on his head. It's possible he slipped and hit a rock, but the wound is consistent with blunt force trauma. Also, I would expect dirt in the wound. This head injury is too clean. And the bruising is all in a straight line. Like whatever he hit his head on had an edge to it. The rocks on this bank are worn smooth and round."

"Who would want to kill a harmless crackpot like Scott?" Rachel asked.

"Another treasure hunter? Maybe one who bought into his theory that your Grampy Coin hid his valuables around here?" Jake scratched his chin. "Last time I talked to Scott, he went on about subterranean caves somewhere around the resort.

"If someone else believed him, they may have thought by killing Scott they could take the treasure for themselves," Rachel said.

"We may as well treat this like a homicide," Jake said. "Bag the hands, wrap him in a tarp and let the state crime lab call it. If there's any proof, they should get back to us in about…six months."

"By then Fort Smith will finish their work and the fall rain will put the possible crime scene under water," Dr. Dave said.

"Unless you get lucky and catch a break with the lab," Rachel said. "So we should expect the lab work this week."

"If the luck comes my way, I won't turn it down. But I never count on it."

Rachel dug through the tool box holding his crime scene kit for his camera, plastic bags, rubber bands and a tarp. Jake hated needing all of this. But after the murders at the hotel during their wedding, he'd decided the city needed an updated crime scene kit.

Under Rachel's direction, Jake steered the boat around the emerging chimney to take photos of Scott Walters's body from all sides. Then they moved closer and photographed his clothing and wounds. Next they placed his hands in plastic bags, spread the tarp over the bottom of the boat and rolled his body onto it. They wrapped it like a burrito. After that Jake examined the "chimney."

"If not for this pipe, we wouldn't have found the body for weeks," Dr. Dave said. "The evidence would've been long gone, then."

"Yeah," Jake said. "We were fortunate." He frowned at the word. Just once, he wished his infamous luck didn't involve finding dead bodies.

Jake turned the boat back toward the shore and the waiting rubberneckers. "I think I'd better commandeer Billy and Emmit from Sarah for a bit longer," he said. "This job just got bigger than I can handle! I need help walking the shore to find where Scott might've fallen, keeping people away from the lake and out of those submerged buildings until we know it's safe and keeping order once people start wandering around down there."

"Hey!" Dr. Dave pointed out at the lake. "Did you see that?"

"What?" Rachel whirled, rocking the boat with her movement.

"I thought I saw a fin!" Dr. Dave said. He leaned forward, hand extended over the water. "Out past the underwater buildings! There was a big fish!"

"I don't see anything," Rachel said.

Dr. Dave squinted at the water. Then shook his head. "It's gone now. But I swear I saw it!"

"Don't tell Horace," Jake said. "On second thought, tell Horace. If he thinks there's a big catfish down here, maybe he'll give me more help policing this area."

Winn stood with Horace and Jimbo at the lake's edge when they beached the boat. The three old men hovered right behind Billy and Emmet, waiting to see the corpse. The two "deputies" caught the prow of the craft and eased it further up the bank. Then they took Rachel's hand and helped her out.

Winn lifted the tarp covering Scott's body. "Yep. Dead. No two ways about it."

"What is that thing out there?" Horace pointed back at the chimney.

"It's the tower of the old resort," Jake said. He cleared his throat and called out to the crowd gathered beyond the barrier. "We won't know if there are any other buildings until the water goes down."

"What about a fish finder or some sonar gizmo?" Jimbo asked. "Bet you we could tell using Winn's pontoon boat."

"How will you get it into the lake, drag it?" Jake waved at the boat ramp, now high and dry above the water line.

Jimbo scratched his head. "Maybe we could buy one and mount it to the John Boat?"

"You offering?" Horace asked.

"I'll make a donation if the city will match me fifty-fifty," Jimbo said.

"Sixty-forty?" Horace countered.

"Are you the sixty?" Jimbo set his jaw.

Horace turned to Jake. "Could you use a fish finder?"

Someone cleared her throat. Jake turned to find Jody and Marco at the edge of the barrier.

"Excuse me?" Jody said. "I couldn't help overhear? Do you need a sonar device? Because we have one?"

"Who is she?" Jimbo whispered.

"I think she used to be engaged to Dr. Dave," Horace said.

"Does she always ask so many questions?" Winn asked.

Horace shrugged. "Maybe."

"You have sonar?" Jake shouted over the old men.

Marco ducked under the police barricade. "We wanted some idea what the terrain down there was like so we could plan out our campground now," he said. "We had the old photos, but those can just take you so far since the vegetation is gone. I wanted a submersible drone, but...funding wouldn't cover it."

"Where's your equipment now?" Jake asked.

"Back on campus in Fayetteville," Marco said. "I could bring it down in the morning with our inflatable raft."

Jake stared at the lake. By morning they would see the top of the tower. If the stone roof of the tower could take their weight, they might use it to stage an exploration of the lakebed by sonar. And if Scott dropped anything significant, Jake could pinpoint it.

"First light is at six a.m. Why don't you meet Rachel and I at the diner about five-thirty?"

"Fine by me," Marco said. "Now if you'll excuse us, we have to work out logistics."

"And I've got a shoreline to walk," Jake said.

Average sat on a rock next to Dr. Dave as Jake spoke to Marco and Jody. The Doc had the same far-away expression on his face that he seemed to get whenever he was near his ex. Average shuddered at the murderous impulses she sensed coming from him.

"Doc?" She touched his shoulder. Dr. Dave blinked in confusion. "Doc? Would you care to rejoin the rest of the world?"

Dr. Dave blushed. "I'm okay," he said. "Just daydreaming."

"Felt to me more like plotting murder," Average said.

Dr. Dave turned white.

"Lighten up, Doc," she said.

"Sorry. I'm not comfortable with the fact I'd like a giant catfish to eat my ex-fiancée like some extra in a movie about sharks, tornadoes and sharks in tornadoes." He put his face in his hands.

"Everyone has fantasies they don't talk about," Average said. "It's a safety valve. You can fantasize about General Custer killing your ex so you don't do anything to her *you* regret." She bit her lip. "You're not thinking about doing something you would regret, are you Doc?"

"What?" Dr. Dave shook his head. "No! That's...No."

"Okay. Just making sure." Average put her hands up. "I'm an empath, not a mind reader. You've just got a lot of scary feelings running around in that chest of yours."

"I'll try to keep them under control." Dr. Dave squinted at his ex. "Hey, Av? Does Jody remind you of anyone?"

Average tilted her head to the side in thought. "She reminds me of Meg Ryan or maybe Reese Whitherspoon in that movie where she wore pink and was a lawyer."

"Not Sharon Stone in *Fatal Attraction* though?"

"I suppose as the new girlfriend I should be jealous. But she seems so cute and mostly harmless," Average said.

"So it's just me then." Dr. Dave hunched his shoulders. "Maybe I should invest in therapy."

"She's your ex," Average said. "I wouldn't worry unless you start fantasizing a more direct role in her death."

"Thanks for the vote of confidence," Dr. Dave said. He glanced at his watch. "Mrs. Paulson said someone around here will turn their ankle while climbing the hill. I should go over there and wait on it to happen."

"I'll go with." Average put her hand in his. The two of them walked across the shoreline toward the gathered crowd.

Tracy S. Morris

Chapter 6

"Good Morning Jake," Sarah said as soon as she walked into the diner. Jake slumped lower on his stool at the counter and groaned.

"Morning, Sarah." He gave her a weak smile in greeting.

She settled next to him and gave him the side-eye. "Do you plan to poach my security guards for much longer? I'm starting to get actual guests. Now that there's a city under the lake, people want to have a balcony seat for the excitement."

Jake groaned. "Billy and Emmet keep showing up at my crime scene. If I don't put them to work, they'll just get in the way. Make sure to tell your tourists they can't go near the lake until it's drained and safe unless I say so. I'm taking no chances with accidents."

"I'm doing what I can, Jake," Sarah said in exasperation. "I can't help it if people jump the hedges and head down the hill. You could send Billy and Emmet back to the hotel when they turn up down there. As it is, I'm paying them to work for you."

"In a way, they're still working for you since they're sending your guests back up to the hotel when they find them," Jake said. "Someone could get hurt and sue the hotel."

"To get legal about it, once our guests leave the grounds we're not responsible for injuries," Sarah said.

"Well, why don't you just cut Billy and Emmet's hours back and schedule each of them to rotate days? That'll keep at least one of them busy and out of my hair."

"And you can put the other one to work," Sarah said. "Good plan, Jake." She nodded in satisfaction.

"Pleasure doing business with you," Jake said under his breath. "I've got to go. I promised to help the documentary maker, Rachel and those archaeologists explore the lake."

"Pleasure, as always," Sarah said.

Jake stood at the center of the tower's roof and noted that the lake had dropped two feet since yesterday. The tower gave no indication of crumbling, so he thought the others could climb up there. Once he waved his approval, Marco, Jody, Rachel and Michael climbed out of the raft.

"Do you think the lake is dropping faster than it should?" Jake asked Marco.

"I've got a consultant from the Corps of Engineers on my dig team I can ask later, but she hasn't been concerned by her readings yet," Marco said. "Why?"

"Just something the boy who died yesterday told me." Jake swiped in dismissal.

Michael held up a copy of a photo taken from the top of the tower. He oriented himself using the hotel so that he stood where the photographer stood to take the photograph. Rachel and Marco moved to see over his shoulder.

"According to this photo," Michael said. "The bank stood about a quarter of a mile down the center of the lake. The rest of this particular building stretches out for about 300 feet that way," he pointed in the direction of the chimney pipe. "And an amphitheater lay about 200 yards the opposite direction. On the other side of it were tennis courts, a park, cabins and the bath house with an indoor pool and a bowling alley."

"Some of the rumors say the time capsule rested somewhere under the amphitheater," Rachel told Marco. "If you guys want to search for it while you're here."

Marco mimed writing with a pen. "We'll make a note of it."

"The townsfolk also built a grist mill further up the valley beside the creek. The general store, post office, and the distillery sat on the other side of the road from the bank," Rachel said. "Between here and there sat a golf course."

"This place was fancy for the Ozarks?" Jody said.

Rachel waved her hand in circles, the gesture taking in the whole valley. "Back before airplanes and the interstate system turned this area into...Flyover country, people came from as far as Kansas City or St. Louis to vacation here.

"Grampy put in a lot of the amenities after his competition built the hotel on the hill," Rachel jerked her thumb in the direction of Sarah's business. "He tried to offer more things they couldn't like the golf course. He sank a lot of his money into the attractions, the debt piled up and there were never enough tourists."

"That couldn't have been very long before they built the dam," Michael said. "Otherwise they couldn't have hushed up his bankruptcy."

"They already needed somewhere to put the reservoir. When he went bankrupt, I'm sure it seemed like the perfect place. They could have their lake for a pittance and help him out at the same time." She rubbed her nose once, sneezed and rubbed it again. Then she made a face. "I miss bladder control."

The others looked at her in disbelief.

"Crap! I said that out loud."

"Let's try out this sonar, then," Jake said quickly. "And while we're here, I'd like to do a little investigating of my own."

He pointed to a spot on shore bound by bright yellow sawhorses. "There's where Billy and Emmet found blood on the rocks yesterday," he said. "I'd like to sweep the lake from there to here with the sonar to see if we pick up any evidence relating to his death."

Jake spared a thought to his luck. *I would appreciate at least one clue to go on.* By the time they found the place where Scott fell into the lake, rubberneckers had already trampled it.

Inconclusive. Contaminated evidence. Useless. Jake thought.

All he had to go on at this point was Dr. Dave's gut instinct and a suspicious head wound. Even then, his best suspects were himself and Rachel, since they last saw Scott alive.

Marco and Jody pulled off their backpacks, placed them on the ground and pulled out various pieces of cable. "This is the hand-held sonar." Marco held up a compact box with handles sticking out of each end. "It sends sound waves down to the bottom of the lake. Whenever it encounters something solid, those sound waves will bounce back up to the camera. The data feeds into the monitor screen at the other end of the cable. We get an image from that." He pulled a portable screen out of Jody's pack. "Jody, Michael and Rachel can stay here to identify landmarks on the readout. Officer Coletrane, you row the boat and I'll use the sonar."

"It's better than outfitting Billy and Emmet in snorkel gear and making them dive around down there. Pity." Jake smiled at the mental image of tying a large rock to Billy's ankles and pushing him off of the corner of the tower. He dismissed the thought and focused instead on climbing into the raft and setting the oars in the oar locks.

"We're limited to the length of the cable," Marco warned.

"Let's take a look at what's around this tower," Jake said. "If the rest of the resort is still there, then the whole town might be, too. After that we can move your end to shore and look for submerged clues from there."

Marco put the sonar in the raft. Then he pushed the craft away from the tower and hopped in at the last second.

"Keep an eye out for General Custer," Rachel joked. "Horace and Jimbo will want to know."

Jake laughed as he worked the oars. Marco turned on the device and fiddled with the controls, leaned over the side and held it underwater. He called back to Jody. "What do you see?"

"There is nothing there?" Jody said.

"You're on the wrong side of the building," Rachel said. "Bring the boat around and see if the roof is down there somewhere."

Jake grunted and worked the right oar to turn the boat in the proper direction. He half-expected the sonar to beep at him like something on television. Instead he heard nothing more than the mechanical white noise hum of machinery in action. They rounded the corner of the building and could see Jody on the tower. Jody clapped her hands at whatever she saw on the screen. "There's something there?" She said. "And it's huge?"

"There we go," Rachel said. "Once the water drops another five feet, we'll be able to see it."

"Amazing!" Marco said. "I'm going to be able to poach half the research assistants in the department for this expedition!"

Jake sighed in relief. The archeologists would police themselves. More people on the dig meant more people to guard the dig. And safety in numbers meant less time he would have to spend protecting people from a potential murderer.

"Row to the other side of the tower and then away from it," Marco said. "Let's see if the amphitheater is intact."

"I'm going to bring 'er around," Jake called out to the people on the tower. "Can you feed me some slack in the cable?"

"I got this." Michael bundled the cable in his arms. "I've worked as a grip for most of my own productions."

"Mr. Moder seems handy," Marco commented.

"Sure. Now," Jake said. "I arrested him the day I met him." Marco blanched, prompting Jake to explain. "His last documentary coincided with my wedding and a murder in that hotel." He nodded toward the *Hotel Des Portiers*.

"He became a suspect in your murder investigation?" Marco asked.

"I arrested him as an accessory. I thought one of his co-workers committed the crime."

"Did they?"

Jake kept rowing. "No. The real murderer already killed her."

"Uh..." Marco's mouth opened and closed like General Custer.

"You don't have to say anything," Jake said. "What with the ghost and the preacher who looked like Santa and the Elvis impersonator in the trekkie ears, it was a strange time. Even for us."

The professor sagged in obvious relief. Then his forehead wrinkled in confusion as he mouthed the words *Elvis impersonator*.

"Guys?" Jody waved at them from the tower.

"It's the amphitheater!" Rachel shouted over Jody. "I can see it pretty clearly!"

"What does it look like?" Jake called back.

"Like a Google Earth of the Coliseum in Rome," Rachel said. "In miniature."

"Would you say it's the biggest thing to ever happen in this little town?" Michael pulled out his little camera and trained it on Rachel. Rachel yanked her hair out of a ponytail, turning to hide her face.

"You know it isn't," she said. "You were here last year for the murders."

Michael clicked off his camera and frowned at Rachel. "I can't put that in my documentary."

"It's the truth," Rachel said.

He huffed. "It couldn't hurt you to stretch the truth a little?"

Rachel studied the monitor over Jody's shoulder. "Jake, something moved past the sonar real fast."

Jake allowed the raft to drift. "Did you see what it was?"

She shook her head. "It was moving too quick."

"It's coming back?" Jody flapped a hand like it was a penguin's flipper to draw their attention.

"Is she asking us or telling us?" Jake leaned closer to Marco to whisper.

"When I figure it out, I'll let you know."

All of a sudden, the raft jolted as if struck from beneath. Jake and Marco both grabbed for the sides of the vessel.

"There?" Jody jumped up and down. She pointed to the emerald water just off to the side of the boat. "Did you see that? It was huge?"

Jake squinted at the murky water. A few swirls broke the glassy surface.

The boat rocked again. Marco cried out at the other end of the raft. Jake's balance slipped as his knees buckled and he fell into the bottom of the boat, Marco on top of him.

"Something pulled the sonar right out of my hands," Marco said.

"Did you see it?" Jake asked.

"No," Marco said. "I felt a tug on the line and I just couldn't hang on."

He crawled past Marco to the end of the boat. At the tower, Rachel, Jody and Michael all struggled to hold onto the monitor and line on their end. The cable stretched taut and quivered between the three of them and the water.

"I've landed fish that don't struggle this much," Michael grunted.

"Fish," Jake said. "General Custer!"

Rachel grunted. All at once the line snapped, sending the three of them tumbling to the roof of the tower. The monitor hit the old concrete once, bounced and shattered.

"Rae?" Jake yelled, standing up in the raft. "Are you and the baby ok?"

"We're fine! I landed on Michael." Rachel held up the monitor so that Jake could see the frayed end of the cable. "This looks like it's been chewed through."

"Somebody tell me that's not a giant catfish?" Jody chewed her nails, her doe eyes wide.

"It could've been General Custer," Rachel said.

"It also could've been deadfall," Michael put a comforting hand on Jody's arm. "That's what they say about the Loch Ness Monster: the currents to kick up old logs that look like a monster. Maybe the sonar got tangled around an old tree trunk."

"And maybe it's a plesiosaur from the Jurassic age," Marco glared at Michael.

"Stranger things have happened," Jake said. He re-set the oars. "We better get to shore before whatever it was comes back."

He rowed the raft up to the tower so the others could climb back in. Rachel stared into the water as if searching for the behemoth fish.

Winn was leaning against the community center's front door when Rachel and Jake pulled up in the truck. The old farmer grinned at them and then started over. A murderous look crossed Rachel's face and she revved her engine.

"Be nice," Jake said. "He's just here to find out if we saw General Custer."

"He started it." Rachel shifted the car into park and crossed her arms. "He ought to be ashamed of himself, picking on Alice. He might as well push her down on the playground and pull on her pigtails."

Jake started at the implication of Winn flirting with his mother-in-law.

Winn knocked on Jake's window and mimicked rolling it down like an old hand-cranked version. "Morning, Jake. Ya'll been out to the lake?"

Jake glanced back at the University's raft in the bed of the truck. "What gave us away?"

"See anything?"

Before Jake could speak, Rachel stopped him with a hand on his chest. "What brings you down to the courthouse, Winn?" She glared at the old farmer. "We haven't needed your services as county coroner since last night."

Winn tucked his hands into his pants pockets. "Just paying off a little fine or two. Doing my part as a law abiding citizen."

Rachel harrumphed. "I need to get over to the clinic, Jake."

Jake opened the car door and slid out. "I'll send Billy and Emmet over to take the raft back."

Rachel sniffed in distain as she drove away. Winn cackled. "She got a bee in her bonnet and make no mistake."

"She's loyal to Alice. Speaking of which, why take things out on my mother-in-law? She hasn't got anything to do with city business and you know I can't cancel your fines. Horace would rather eat his own liver."

"It's the principle of the thing," Winn sniffed. "I'm trying to go legitimate by making soap 'stead of 'shine. If I could get out from underneath those fines..." He let the sentence hang.

"Legitimate?" Jake put his hands on his hips. "You?"

"S'true," Winn cleared his throat. "Mabel done made me promise on her death bed that I'd reform. She said I'm bein' a bad influence on the grandkids. It's all fine and dandy if I raise llamas or make soap. But no more corn mash. I could pay off the fines with the coroner job if we got another string of murders like last year. But other than last night, the dyin' business has been slow."

Jake clicked his teeth as he thought it over. If Winn got rid of his still, it would remove most of the bootleg liquor in Tranquility. "What if I let you work off the fines?"

"Like community service?"

"Exactly," Jake said. "I need some additional help keeping people from poking around the ruins in the lake. Billy and Emmet are eager, but--"

"The elevator don't go all the way to the top." Winn cackled.

"Since you're searching for General Custer anyways, you could keep an eye on things. Horace won't object. I'd bet he would pay for it himself."

"Not in actual dollars," Winn said.

"This is close enough," Jake said. "Horace loves this kind of mutual trade out."

Winn spat in his hand and they shook on it. As the old man started to pull away, Jake gripped his hand tighter. "You are going to bury the hatchet with Alice, aren't you?"

"Is she going to bury the hatchet with me, or in my back?" Winn asked, a gleam of admiration in his eye. "She's a stubborn woman."

Jake glared at Winn. "It would help if you made up a batch of soap for her."

"It's going to take a bit," Winn said. "I've got an order in for lard, but my supplier can't deliver 'til sometime next week."

"Can't you just go into Fort Smith and get some from a butcher?"

Winn opened his mouth in an "O" of horror. "Oh no, Jake! I can't get fat just anywhere. Trade secret, you know."

"Alright," Jake held his hands up in surrender. "I won't ask." He really didn't want to think about Winn's fat anyway.

"You mentioned General Custer earlier," the old farmer said.

Jake waved for Winn to follow him into the building. "Something strange happened up at the lake today." He described the incident with the vanishing sonar. Winn hummed thoughtfully as Jake finished.

Jake sat at his desk as the old farmer eased into the seat across from him. "So what do you think?"

"That don't sound like behavior coming from no stick of wood I've ever heard of." Winn coughed, pulled a red bandanna from his pocket and spit into it. "That old resort still in one piece down there would explain why we never could find General Custer no matter how many times we fished the lake. I bet he hid out in them fancy buildings the whole time."

"What happened seemed like something out of Shark Week."

Winn nodded in agreement. "We better warn people. It sounds like General Custer is getting cranky."

"Cranky?" Jake fought to keep his face neutral.

"Your home drying up would make you a might techy too. If we're not careful, someone else could get hurt."

"That's assuming Scott just fell into the lake and wasn't murdered." Jake took off his hat and rubbed the top of his head. "My concern is that someone might get stuck in those ruins and drown while exploring. But if you see anyone out there poking around, please call me instead of trying to chase them off yourself."

"Will do." Winn stood. "Now if you'll excuse me. I'm headed to the drugstore. Jimbo is going to want to know that General Custer is getting all out of sorts."

A new thought occurred to Jake. "Winn?"

Winn froze in his tracks. "Yeah, Jake?"

"You wouldn't be thinking about flushing General Custer out of his hiding spot with dynamite, would you?"

"Now Jake, why would I do that?" He shuffled back and forth on his feet.

"I wonder," Jake said. "Don't drop anything explosive into the lake." He stroked his chin, wondering whether he covered everything with that statement. With Winn, you had to close every loophole. "And don't ram the buildings with the boat. Or try to pull them down with a tow chain. Don't do anything that could damage those buildings, the university-types want to study them.

"Well, dang! What does that leave us?" Winn scratched his head.

"Just stop trying to flush him out," Jake said. "If he's there, he's already running out of places to hide. A cornered animal is more dangerous, anyway."

"If you say so." Winn's shoulders slumped. He looked like a whipped puppy as he left.

Jake opened his browser and typed in the words *giant catfish*. Then he sat back and drummed his fingers on his desk. The sound of footsteps heralded Average's arrival. She could doubtless sense his annoyance at the old, slow machine, and at her father for refusing to replace it. She probably even sympathized.

"eBay?" She asked.

"Research on giant catfish," Jake said. "Why did you think eBay?"

"I passed Winn on the way in here. He said General Custer ate your sonar."

"It's the university's sonar. I don't think the city has to pay for it, since the archaeologists were using the equipment to plan their dig and we were just along for the ride." Slow as molasses, the search engine retrieved his results. Jake leaned forward and Average moved around the desk to stare over his shoulder.

"Grizzly Bear sized catfish caught in Thailand," Jake read. He clicked on the link, which showed a catfish the size of a man laid out across a rowboat. Average let out a low whistle. "Mekong giant catfish can reach ten feet long and weigh up to 650 pounds."

"So it's possible something like General Custer can exist."

"Yeah, but that's in Thailand," Jake said.

"Dad said that some soldier brought General Custer over from China."

Jake grunted. He backed out of the page and looked over the links again. "Shark found in the Mississippi River near Alton, Illinois."

"What?" Average leaned closer to the screen.

"This article dates back to 1937. It's a fluke," Jake said.

"No, I'm pretty sure it's a shark."

"I meant an abnormality."

"We never see those in Tranquility, either," she chided.

Jake ignored her. "Giant Catfish in India turn to preying on humans."

"Not like any catfish I ever caught," Average said.

"They're from Eurasia," Jake said. "Says here the wels catfish will attack swans, but they leave people alone. The goonch of India is a whole 'nother story. The Indian people bury their dead in their rivers and the catfish eat the bodies. They get big and fat and develop a taste for people."

"Yuck!" Average shuddered.

"At least we know it's possible, even if it's not likely." He tapped the screen, where he'd scrolled onto an image of two men straining under the weight of an enormous, bloated fish. "I'm glad I didn't send Billy into the lake with a snorkel, now."

"Should I pass the word around the diner?" Average tilted her head sideways.

Jake leaned back in his chair and rubbed his hands together. "Do it. We may as well make the rumor work for us. If people think they could get eaten by a giant catfish, they'll stay out of the water and away from the ruins. At least for a while."

"Ya'll getting attacked by the catfish ended up being lucky."

"Looks like." Jake pressed his lips together.

Chapter 7

Dr. Dave sat at a table with Jody when Jake and Average entered the diner.

"...So then I told Daddy I would rather die than wear chartreuse? I don't care if Lynette chose it for her wedding color? If she wants me as her maid of honor, she would totally listen to me and change it?"As Jody spoke, she waved her hands in the air like she was directing a plane toward a gate.

The Doc wore a dazed expression, as if Jody snuck up behind him and clubbed him like a baby seal.

That may be how she gets people to sit and listen to her, Jake thought. While he watched, the Doc grasped a fork in both hands and bent it into a U-shape.

Jake tugged on Average's sleeve and jerked his chin at the Doc. "Is he alright?"

Average huffed. "He's not coping with seeing his ex. I know how to snap him out of it." She retrieved a coffee cup and pot from behind the counter, filled one with the other and slammed them down on the table in front of Dave. Both the doctor and Jody jumped as the hot liquid fountained up from the mug and splattered all over the table. Then the waitress took the bent fork out of Dr. Dave's hands. "You ought to stay away from things that cause you to bend forks, Uri Gellar." She took the utensel with her as she left.

"What's that all about?" Jake asked as he sat down at the table.

"I'm sure it's just jealousy?" Jody tossed her hair over her shoulder. "I deal with this all the time?"

"You don't say," Jake mumbled to be polite as he leaned back and stared at Dr. Dave for a better explanation. The Doc avoided his eyes by mopping at the stains on the table with a paper napkin.

Just then, Jody stood and waved at the door like a Disney princess on a float. "There's Marco? Marco? Over here?"

Two blonde women, one of them short and apple-shaped with a beak-like nose and the other tall and built like a scarecrow, followed Marco through the door into the restaurant. The tall girl wore her hair in pigtails and both women wore straw cowboy hats. As they spotted Jody, they each made an expression that reminded Jake of the first time his son tried strained peas.

"David? Let me introduce you to my team?" Jody said. Both women's jaws dropped.

"Her team?" The taller blonde rounded on Marco. "What does she mean by *her team?*" The shorter woman crossed her arms and glared, reminding Jake of an angry bluebird.

Marco pinballed from Jody to each of the other women in a desperate search for safety. "The team..." He worked his jaw as if he could catch the words from the air. Then his face lit in sudden inspiration. "The team she's a part of. Just like the rest of us. Her team."

He grasped Jody's shoulder. "We should check the equipment," he said with a nervous laugh. "You two should introduce yourselves to Officer Coltrane. He rowed the boat with me when the lake monster ate the camera. I'm sure he would love to tell you all about it."

Without waiting for an answer, Marco pulled Jody from the diner.

"What a coward!" The Angry Bluebird spat, sitting in Jody's vacated seat.

"He has to keep this year's model with him at all times to keep her from screwing up the dig," The Scarecrow shook her head. "I swear, they get dumber each season. This one thinks she's in charge and he doesn't even bother to correct her."

"That's what he gets for thinking with the wrong brain," Angry Bluebird replied. "I wish she would just hurry up, get her MRS degree and go home."

"Jody's not in college for a husband," Dr. Dave said at last. Both women turned to him with speculative expressions.

"How do you know?" Scarecrow asked.

"I'm her ex-fiancée," Dr. Dave said. "And even if he—" The Doc broke off to wave at the door where Marco went. "Tried correcting her it wouldn't matter. Jody only hears what she wants to hear."

"You're David," Scarecrow said. "Seems like you're all she talks about."

"The guy who left her at the altar?" The Angry Bluebird asked. She peered at each of Dr. Dave's hands. "I always thought you chewed off your own arm to get away from her."

"It didn't get quite that far," Dr. Dave smiled like he had gas. He pointed to Jake. "Meet Officer Coletrane."

"I'm Margaret Wilde, but you can call me Maggie." The Angry Bluebird pointed to herself. Then she jerked her thumb in the direction of Scarecrow. "Samantha Dupree. Our Consultant from the Corps of Engineers."

"Call me Sandy. Is there an actual lake monster?" Sandy asked. "I thought Marco made it up."

Jake shrugged. "Local legends say it's a giant catfish. The fishermen even have a name for him: General Custer. But my wife would be the expert on the subject."

"A fish ate our equipment. Great," Maggie said. "This is not worth six credits."

"We could always just blame it on Jody," Sandy said.

"I don't think Marco would let us get away with shifting the blame to *Little Miss Answers Must Be In The Form Of A Question*," Maggie snapped. She whirled on Dr. Dave. "Do you ever have fantasies that you want to kill her just like Danny DeVito in that movie?"

The Doc blushed. "Danny DeVito? Like in *Drowning Mona*?" He released a nervous laugh.

"No, like in *Throw Mama from the Train*. In *Drowning Mona* he was a cop and everyone else in town wanted to kill Bette Midler."

"Fantasize all you want," Jake cut in. "But that's where it stops. We keep our town quiet." Then he thought about the murders at the wedding and the problems with the Big Bird. "Most of the time."

"People here don't know Jody very well yet," Dr. Dave said.

"She seems harmless at first," Sandy put in. "But it's little things that get to you. She cleaned Marco's office and lost our research before he could compile it into a report."

"She told the wife of my attending physician at the hospital she shouldn't wear A line dresses because they made her look dowdy," Dr. Dave said. "I wound up scheduled onto midnight rotations for six months."

"She tightened the holes in the mesh screens we use to grade soil into sizes because 'stuff fell through.'" Maggie tilted back her cowboy hat and scratched her hairline. "At best she seems inept. At worst…"

"Stupid," Sandy concluded.

"Passive-aggressive and good at hiding it," Dr. Dave added.

"I'm not sure anyone is that good at acting," Maggie said. "I don't even think she knows she's doing it." She shook her head in dismissal. "But you know what they say: Can't live with her, can't bury her under the porch. Bless her little heart."

Jake looked at Maggie in alarm. But the short woman blinked at him, all innocence, as if to say: *I'm being funny and precious, so what are you going to do about it?*

Maggie took Sandy's hand. "We should catch up to Marco and The Princess before she punches a hole in our raft."

"Heaven help us." Sandy made a wry face.

Once the two women left, Jake asked Dr. Dave: "Do you think Jody might have some kind of talent or power like the kind we have here in Tranquility?"

Dr. Dave hummed. "Is there any test for that?"

"Sorry, no," Jake said. "But those two women act like they want to kill your ex. And it don't fit with what I saw of Jody. If she has some kind of gift to make folk dislike her, it might explain it."

"She's got a gift for it, alright," Dr. Dave said. "I don't think it has much to do with the kind of gift you, Average and Rachel have."

"I'll feel better when the lake comes back and all these archaeologists go home." Jake pointed at Dr. Dave. "Until then, mind some advice?"

"Sure." Dr. Dave lowered his head.

"Jody bothers you, too. So avoid her."

Dr. Dave let out a weak laugh. "I'd like to. She's very clingy for an ex."

"Then try not to let her get you alone. Average can help."

The Doc made moon eyes at Average. "Sounds like a win-win for me."

Chapter 8

"What's all this?" Rachel stood on the earthen dam overlooking the lake. The university archaeologists had set up their camp on the hillside between the ruins and the *Hotel des Portiers*. The archaeologists now seemed like worker ants busy digging in the soil. "I thought they wouldn't be able to dig up anything until the lake finished draining,"

Michael Moder turned to the two people on his camera crew. "Karl, April, either of you know what's going on?" He waved at the archaeologists.

April nodded. "I spoke with Professor Casari on the phone this morning," she said. "They found a midden pile yesterday evening."

"Midden?" Rachel scratched her head.

"Trash pile," April supplied.

"Did you know about any trash piles your uncle may have used?" Michael asked Rachel.

"It's not like my kin kept up with every single little dump site Grampy Coin had. It makes sense, though. Mom always said Grampy Coin hated the *Hotel des Portiers*. Of course he would've thrown his trash out right where it would spoil their view."

Michael grabbed Karl's arm. Once he had the cameraman's attention, he took in the entire valley with a wave of his free hand. "Get a panning shot of all of this," he said.

After Karl finished taking his footage, the four of them walked across the dam to the campsite. As they neared the spot where Maggie worked, a foul stench rolled over Rachel like a semi-truck, churning up her stomach in the process. She threw herself to her knees with the shamelessness of a teen singing sensation at a music awards after party, and left her last meal on the side of the path.

The others looked at Rachel in surprise, then the smell hit them. "Eugh!" April's face twisted in disgust. She held her nose and tried to wave the smell away from herself. "Where is that stink coming from?"

"Hey Preggo!" Maggie glared up from a shallow pit carved in a perfect square. From her vantage point, Rachel could see the archaeologist scraping away dirt layer-by-layer with a trowel. She frowned an angry bluebird scowl at them. "If you know you're going to up-chuck, carry around a barf bag. You don't see me throwing up all over the place where you work."

"Sorry," Rachel ducked her head.

"She can't help it." Karl clamped his sleeve to his nose. "Your camp stinks."

"I blame Marco's princess." Maggie jerked her trowel up as if wielding a knife. The tip of the tool pointed back toward two domed-shaped tents. "She's the one who chose our campsite." Before Maggie could say more, Marco and Jody walked up.

"The documentary film-makers! Welcome! Welcome!" Marco clapped his hands together in enthusiasm. "How can we help you to get started?"

"I thought to interview you today on what you hoped to find here?" Marco pointed at Karl's camera.

"Of course?" Jody elbowed her way in front of Marco. The professor gave her the stink-eye as Jody preened. "I can tell you anything you need to know, but you'll need to get my best side?"

For once, Marco seemed annoyed at Jody. Michael's gaze ping-ponged from the professor to Jody and back like a swimmer plotting a path through shark-infested waters.

"Professor, can you show April and myself around?" The director asked. "We can get plenty of b-roll footage. Karl, why don't you and Mrs. Coletrane stay here and interview Jody?"

Rachel's jaw dropped. What did she know about interviewing anyone? Michael just threw her under a bus for the sake of getting away. Before she could protest, Michael and April hot-footed it away with Marco. Karl shrugged at her and then pointed his camera at Jody.

"Sooooo," Rachel drew the word out while scrambling for the questions to ask. "How...did you decide where to camp?" She winced at the lousy question. What did it have to do with the dig? Other than making everyone who worked here miserable?

"I followed an omen?"

"Are you superstitious?" Rachel tilted her head. "What kind of omen?"

"I knew this stench meant something, you know?" Jody said. "So I poked around with a shovel and I found this?" She produced a large piece of wood and held it up so Karl could film it. Someone in the past carved a crescent moon into the center of the plank.

Rachel sucked in a breath in surprise, forgetting about the smell. She coughed and spluttered, trying to force the foul air back out.

"You do...she coughed again. "You do know what it means, right?"

Jody grinned and pointed to the *Hotel des Porters* on the hill. "They use a crescent moon on their signs? So this must be from there?"

"Right." Rachel decided not to mention that it also indicated an outhouse. Which meant the smell saturating the camp came from an old privy, and the 'midden' piles weren't trash piles, but antique crap piles. Theoretically, ancient crap shouldn't stink. But in Tranquility anything was possible.

Behind Jody, Maggie lunged with her trowel raised as a makeshift club. Before she could connect, Sandy threw herself on Maggie to hold her back.

"Let me at her," Maggie cajoled in a voice Rachel could just hear. "You could help me, Sandy! You know you want to."

"Not here!" Sandy shot back. "Too many witnesses!"

Just then Marco, Michael and April returned.

"Ladies!" Marco interrupted them before they could shed blood. "Why don't you sort and catalog the broken bottles and crockery you found this morning?"

"I already did?" Jody chirped. She smiled in pride and stood a little straighter.

Sandy wore a dangerous expression. "When?" She put her hands on her hips.

"After I got back from the hotel?"

"The hotel?" Maggie shone her hostile expression on Marco. The professor gulped and tugged at his collar.

"Um..." He took a step backward.

"How many hotels have you seen in this town? *The* hotel?" Jody pointed up the hill to the *Hotel des Portiers.* "Marco said the two of us should have a command center so we can plan and strategize this dig?"

"And I suppose you slept there instead of your tent?" Maggie sneered.

"Yeah?" Jody scratched her head. "Why would I waste a bed?"

Sandy joined Maggie in staring down Marco. To Jody she asked: "What did you do to the potsherds?"

"I washed them?" Jody puffed out her chest a bit more. "I even glued them back together?"

Maggie buried her face in her hands. Sandy grasped Maggie's shoulder. "I'm going to take Maggie and see if we can salvage our work." She threw one more angry glare Marco's way and pushed Maggie ahead of her as she shuffled away.

"Wow? They're too overcome to thank me? Think how excited they'll be when we find the time capsule?"

"Maybe we should offer them the use of our shower and the pull-out sofa?" Marco sounded a little frightened for his own safety.

Jody tilted her head like a curious baby seal. "Why? They brought their bed rolls, didn't they? And someone needs to guard the camp?" She spread her hands wide and knocked the camera out of Karl's hands. The machinery hit the ground once and bounced, releasing ominous sparks.

Mark, April and Karl all covered their mouths, eyes wide. Karl was the first to unfreeze from his horrified pose. He picked up the camera and turned it over in his hands. "I think you fried the memory." He slumped. "We just lost a week's worth of footage. All we have is the b-roll on the other camera."

"Oopsie?" Jody winced. "I didn't see you there?"

"Oopsie!" Michael said through clenched teeth. "All you can say is Oopsie?"

Jody seemed confused as to why Michael suddenly turned hostile. "I'm sorry? You know, you just filmed my interview and now it's lost too? I'm suffering for my mistake, same as you are?"

"Not yet, you're not…" Michael broke off as April and Rachel both jumped between him and Jody.

"Let's go, Michael." April sounded tired. "I'll start re-booking your other interviews."

Jody made the universal sign for telephone. "Give me a call when you want to re-do mine?"

"Riiiiight," April huffed, then led the camera crew plus Rachel up the hill away from the dig site. When Rachel looked back, Marco shook his finger at Jody while she held her hands in the air waving them, each of them trying to out-yell the other.

"Grandma! There's someone coming up the driveway!" Tommy yelled.

Tommy had hooked his knees over the top of the couch, hanging upside down off of the backside, facing out the window. "Tommy? What have I told you about climbing on the couch?"

"I should at least clean the windows while I'm back here," Tommy recited.

"Good boy." Alice set her knitting down and walked to the window. "Can you see who it is?"

"It's Mr. Stevens."

Alice harrumphed. "Why don't you run off to your room to play?"

"Are you going to say things Dad and Rachel wouldn't want me to hear?" Tommy asked.

"You can bet on it."

"Aw, man." Tommy grumbled as he pulled himself upright onto the couch. "If I don't get to hear you say them, how am I ever going to fund my swear jar?"

"How does the jar work?" Alice asked as she watched Winn walk up her porch steps.

"A quarter per cuss word," Tommy said.

Alice pulled her mad money from her bra and handed Tommy a twenty dollar bill. "That should cover anything I have to say to Winthrop Stevens."

Tommy's face lit up like it was Christmas. He took the money and dashed up her stairs sounding like a herd of elephants.

She moved to her door to wait for Winn's knock. She jerked the door open a second before it came. Then she crossed her arms. "Well?"

"Afternoon, Mrs. Alice," Winn gave her his possum-eating grin.

"I believe you are correct. That is the time of day." Alice tilted her head, regal as any southern belle half her age. "I'm surprised to have you on my doorstep, given our recent unpleasantries."

"About that," Winn mopped at his forehead with his annoying red bandanna and looked at her with a hopeful expression. Alice frowned. Every instinct she possessed told her to shut the door in his face. But her own mother would literally come back to haunt her if she behaved as less than a lady.

"Why don't you come in?" She stepped aside. "I'm sure I have some lemonade in the fridge."

Winn sat at her Formica table while she poured him a drink. Then she took the chair across from him and drummed her fingers as she waited for him to get to the point. To her annoyance Winn tilted his chair back. "I suppose I should stop hem-hawing around."

"That would be nice." She lifted an eyebrow at the way the chair creaked and groaned under his weight.

"Right." He cleared his throat. "I talked to Jake."

She glanced up in the direction of Tommy's room. At this rate, her grandson would be sneaking down the stairs just as she worked herself into a good frothing tirade. "And?"

"We worked things out between us man-to-man. We've got an understanding now. So I guess you can buy my soap again."

"That's all you have to say to me?" Her blood boiled.

Winn shrugged. "Well, I wanted to wait a month or two before I asked you out. But I suppose we could go to the drive-in up in Fayetteville this Saturday night."

Her temper snapped. "I would sooner dig up my late husband, God rest his soul, and take him to the drive-in than go with you, Winthrop Stevens!"

Winn's jaw dropped. He sat his lemonade down hard enough for the liquid to slosh over the sides.

"What's wrong with you, woman? I said things were fine now."

"Did you ask me if things were fine between *us*?" Alice snapped. "You made me a pawn in a sad attempt to manipulate my son-in-law. Did you think to apologize to me? Did I get any consideration for my feelings?"

"Well I asked you out," Winn said.

"You may think you're a catch as good as General Custer, but you're just a tiny perch stuck to a trot line. And furthermore, you sit on my furniture right! You're a guest in my house! Behave like one!" She then blistered the air with a stream of cursing worth every penny of the twenty dollars she'd just given to Tommy. When she ran out of curse words, she invented new ones. After she finished, she pointed to the door. "Now I think you better leave!"

Winn looked like he couldn't figure out quite where he lost control of the conversation. Then his face twisted in anger. "Fine! Stubborn, prideful woman!" He muttered several choice words as he walked out the door.

As soon as he left, Tommy stuck his head back in the room. "Does the money you gave me cover what Mr. Stevens said on his way out?"

"No, it doesn't," Alice said.

"Cool!" Tommy grinned. "I'm telling dad!"

Chapter 9

David heard soft, feminine snuffling sounds outside his front door. Then someone knocked.

Jody, David thought. It felt like a weight on his chest. He considered sneaking out the back. Or at least going into his bedroom with his reports, shutting the door and pretending he wasn't home.

"D...David?" She sobbed. "I know you're home? P...Please let me in?"

He let his head fall forward, then shook it, not quite able to believe the situation. Then he got up and opened the front door just enough to see outside.

Jody stood on the mat: eyes puffy, nose red, shoulders slumped.

David shut the door and scratched his head in confusion. What happened to the woman who looked like Sharon Stone's twin? He opened the door to take a second look at her.

Jody peered up at him with a sad puppy expression, sniffed once and hiccoughed. "Ca...Can I come in?" Her breath hitched.

David shut the door in her face. He thought about calling Average and asking her what to do. But Average had her hands full closing the diner tonight. He sketched the sign of the cross. One brief touch to his forehead, chest and then each shoulder. He wasn't Catholic, but how could it hurt? Then he opened the door wide to invite the soul-sucking vampire in.

"Thanks, David?" Jody offered a watery smile. She slipped past him like he might change his mind if she hesitated, threw herself onto his naugahyde sofa, curled into a tight ball and tucked her knees under her chin.

"Needy, soul-sucking vampire. Awesome." He muttered as he sat on the other end of the couch and stared at her like she might sprout fangs and attack him at any minute. "What's wrong, Jo?"

"You haven't called me that in forever?"

David shrugged.

Jody nodded, her expression distant in thought. "Am I selfish?"

David dropped his head to the back of the couch. *That's a loaded question,* he thought. *'Am I selfish? Does this dress make me look fat? If I died, would you get married again?' Every time I answered those types of questions, she threw me out...*

He realized she couldn't throw him out of his own house. Or the city's house he lived in.

"Yes," David said. "Yes you are."

Jody's face fell. "Really?"

"Little bit." He held his hand so the tips of his thumb and forefinger were an inch apart to demonstrate. Then he shut one eye. From this perspective, Jody's head fit between his two fingers. He pinched them together as if squishing it like a grape over and over.

"What are you doing?" She pulled her mouth into a lopsided V.

"Nothing." David put his hand back on the couch.

She hid her face in her hands. "The others said some awful things about me?"

"Why ever would they do that?" He put both hands to his face, sarcasm dripping from every word.

"I don't know?" She wailed. "They seemed mad that Marco and I had a hotel room and they didn't?"

David pinched the bridge of his nose. He used to hope she would just get a clue on her own. But now...Why shouldn't he just hit her between the eyes with a clue-by-four?

"Why did you get a hotel?" He asked.

"We needed a command center?"

"But why did you sleep there instead of with your group at their campsite?"

"Because I didn't want to sleep on the ground?" Jody said.

"When you and your boyfriend got your own hotel, did you think the others might want a room also?" David led her through his reasoning.

Jody wrinkled her nose like a confused rabbit.

He decided to try again. "What about this?" He waved to his own living room. "You and I haven't seen each other since we broke up. Yet you showed up on my doorstep the second you got into town. Don't you think that might be a little bit uncomfortable?"

"I'm fine with it," Jody said.

"I'm not!" David snapped. "And the people we're seeing now might not like it, either! Stop thinking of just yourself,"

She squinted in comprehension. "You're not?"

"Not so much," David said.

She pointed at him, as if having a Eureka moment. "*That's* why you broke things off with me? You were hurt because I didn't think of you before going on a date?"

"Give the little lady a cigar," David said.

Something in Jody's expression sharpened. "I've got a lot to think about?"

"Ya' think?" David asked. He just wanted her to go away, but that didn't seem likely. But he *could* leave. A plan formed in his mind. He pointed to his bedroom. "Would you like to borrow my room? I'm going to go see my girlfriend."

Jody appeared uncertain. "You would leave me alone? You could just stay here. . . On the couch?"

"No," David shook his head. "I couldn't. My girlfriend is a priority in my life." He left unspoken the fact that Jody wasn't.

"Oh...okay?" She rolled from the couch and walked to his room. She took a deep, steadying breath. "I'll just let myself out in the morning?"

David relaxed when the door closed. Then he tensed right back up. Jody might come back out of his bedroom any minute with another needy request.

As quietly as he could, he gathered up his paperwork, put it in his briefcase, grabbed his keys and ran for the door as if all the demons of hell chased after him.

The tips of one story roofs peeked out from the surface of Lake Tranquility. Moonlight created a silver ribbon that twisted around the tips of the rooftops as they emerged from the depths of the lake. The night seemed to have its own music which included the chirp of frogs, the hum of cicadas, and tonight, Jimbo's deep, booming cackle.

On Winn's pontoon boat out in the center of the lake, Jimbo held his sides as he doubled over in laughter.

Behind the boat's wheel, Winn crossed his arms and stared at Jimbo. "Ain't funny," he said.

"Sure it is," Jimbo grinned. "I could'a told you that you were wastin' your time askin' Alice on a date. Not while she's still talkin' to her dead husband."

"Why would you want to date her, anyhow?" Horace scratched his head. "At our age, you'd get hitched by Christmas. And she knows where too many of the bodies got buried, if you take my meanin'."

"Of course she knows where all the bodies went," Jimbo said. "She talks to all of them."

"I mean, you can't hide anything from her," Horace threw his hands up.

"Because the dead relatives you ticked off tell her everything," Jimbo said. "You ever decide to get back into the 'shine business, and she'll know it before you gather up enough corn to make a decent mash."

"I kept my soap recipe a secret from her. I can hide anything else."

"You ain't living in the same house as that woman yet," Jimbo said.

"We're gettin' off track here," Winn said. "I didn't get those two idjut wannabe cops from the hotel to drag this pontoon boat down to the water just so the two of you could laugh at me."

"You let Billy and Emmet touch this boat?" Horace sat up in his seat. "We'll be lucky if we don't sink!"

"I watched them real careful to make sure they didn't bang it up!" Winn snapped. "You want to find General Custer before the lake dries up? Or do you want to sit here and give me crap?"

"I could have razzed you back at the diner," Horace said. "Turn on the fish finder."

Winn switched on the machine. Soon a series of beeps filled the air.

"Does that thing have a visual display?" Jimbo asked.

Winn turned the display around so Jimbo could see it. "If you see the fish on the screen, it means there's a fish under the boat. Horace, you want to work the trolling motor?"

Horace moved up past the safety rail to the front of the boat and knelt out of sight.

As he worked, Winn could hear metallic thumps, peppered with the kind of language that would make Jake's son Tommy ask for a quarter. At last, the quiet electric hum of the trolling motor kicked in and the boat drifted forward.

"Remember the first time we saw General Custer, Horace?" Jimbo asked once they got underway. "We played hooky from school and poled a John Boat way back up Lost Spaniard cove?"

"I remember. General Custer bit the ends off our poles and flipped our boat over," Horace said. "We swam back to the bank and walked home. Mama tanned my hide. And we were lucky that fish didn't eat us."

Winn barked in laughter. "My pappy took me fishing first time I ever saw the General." He hawked and spit in the lake. "Pappy liked to fish usin' a stick o' dynamite. We situated ourselves on the bank over the Old Bottomless Hole, and the General came right up to the surface and spit the stick right back at us. Pappy swore the general was trying to drive us into the lake for a bite to eat of his own."

The three men chuckled right up until the moment the front corner of the pontoon bucked.

Horace and Jimbo wore identical horrified expressions. Winn tapped the display of the fish finder, then slapped the side of the screen.

"Log," he said.

Horace put a hand to his chest in relief.

The fish finder chirped.

"School of fish," Winn leaned over the display and squinted at it in the dim glow of the boat's tiki party lights.

"A school of fish, or one big fish? Can your machine tell the difference?" Horace asked.

"How should I know?" Winn snapped back. "I've never tried to find General Custer this way before.

"Never?" Horace threw his hands up. "You didn't mention that before."

"You didn't seem to care," Winn said.

The boat rocked again.

"Let's get out of here a'fore General Custer sucks the boat down!" Jimbo shouted.

"Right!" Winn waved for Horace to pull the trolling motor back up. Then he switched the outboard motor on and cranked up the throttle. The pontoon boat surged forward, then rocked to a violent stop with one corner of the decking up in the air. All three of the old men fell from their seats. The motor stalled, then sputtered out.

Jimbo leaned over the side of the boat. "I think that *school of fish* might've been a big rock. Kind of like the one we're wedged on top of right now."

"Great," Winn said. He cranked the motor, but it refused to start. Winn put his head down against the steering wheel. "Anyone want to swim ashore?"

Horace held up both hands, palms outward and shook his head. "Are you kidding me? That's what General Custer wants! If I get out of this boat, he'll get me!'

"He's got a point," Jimbo said.

"Then we may as well get comfortable." Winn sat back in his captain's chair and crossed his arms. "Cause it's going to be a long wait."

"Now I wish I brought a deck of cards," Jimbo said.

"Doc!" Grab an apron and a pot and start filling coffee cups!" Average called out as soon as David walked in the door.

David looked around in confusion. Customers sat at every table and booth in the diner, waiting for service with sour expressions on their faces.

"Where's your dad?" he asked.

Average shook her head, a rueful expression on her face. "When I got here for my shift, I found the place locked up tight with a line out into the parking lot. Jake ambled in about a half-hour ago and let me know he saw my dad out on the lake this morning."

"That's not like your dad," David said.

"Not on purpose. He, Jimbo and Winn went out on Winn's pontoon boat last night searching for General Custer. Those three old codgers got their boat good and stuck. Jake's down there now rescuing them with the city boat."

David tied on a spare apron, picked up a full pot of coffee and looked around. Mrs. Paulson, his precognitive receptionist, sat in a corner booth with a dictionary, pen and paper.

"I'm playing scrabble with Alice tonight," she said.

"Good morning, Mrs. Paulson. What are you doi...nevermind."

"Yes," she added.

"Coffee?" David asked—using just enough words to ensure she could—or will have—or would have understood him. He filled her cup and then walked back to the counter.

"Is Mrs. Paulson cheating at future scrabble?" He jerked his chin in the direction of the older woman.

"Yes," Average said. "But Alice cheats too. She gets Tennessee Williams to help her with the word tiles."

"Does it help?"

"No," Average said. "He's a writer. So he keeps making up words."

Marco stood on the bank of the lake and waved at Jake as the officer ferried Winn, Jimbo and Horace to shore.

Jake waved back, then resumed his conversation with Winn. "Sorry about your boat. I'm sure you can get it in a week or two when the lake dries up."

"Thanks, Jake," Winn said. "Can you do me one more favor?"

"What?" Jake asked.

"Don't tell Alice," Winn said. Up in the nose of the boat, Horace and Jimbo guffawed.

"Do I want to know why?" Jake asked.

"I doubt it," Horace said. "Hope you don't mind if we don't wait on you, Jake. But Jimbo and I need to get back and mind the store."

"Fine," Jake waved them off as the boat beached.

"Good morning, Officer." Marco grabbed the end of the craft to steady it.

"You're out early," Jake said to Marco as he helped Winn out of the boat.

"I can't find Jody," the professor explained. "The girls all got into it last night. Jody got her feelings hurt and took off."

Jake grunted. He bet that the other girls finally got too catty with Jody and Marco didn't stop them.

"Have you checked the diner? Sooner or later, everyone turns up there."

"Not yet," Marco said. "I'm sure she's fine. She may've just gone home to Fayetteville." He sounded hopeful.

"Could be," Jake said.

Chapter 10

The diner was so empty by the time Jake entered that lint balls the size of tumbleweeds could have rolled down the aisles and no one would have noticed. Average and Dr. Dave sat in one of the booths. Dr. Dave rested his head on the table in exhaustion while Average curled into a ball on the space next to him.

"Did Horace make it back?" Jake asked.

"He's in the kitchen." Average uncurled and wriggled out of the booth. "Do you want your usual?"

"Just coffee today." Jake held up a thermos. "I need to make the rounds." He sat in the booth across from Dr. Dave and waited while she returned with a decanter to fill his thermos.

"Hope your dad gives you the afternoon off after what happened," Jake said.

"Hah!" Average scoffed as she sat again. "Is he giving *you* the day off?"

"Didn't think he would," Jake rolled his eyes.

"All three of us are on the city clock today," Dr. Dave said.

Jake remembered his conversation with Marco. "Either one of you see Jody today? Her boyfriend said she didn't go back to camp last night."

"She's at my house," Dr. Dave said.

"Is that so?" Jake narrowed his eyes.

"Dr. Dave spent the night on my couch." Average draped her arm over his shoulders. "Jody showed up on his doorstep last night seeking comfort. He let her have his place because she had nowhere to go."

"Pretty smart on your part, Doc," Jake said.

"When you give advice, I know to take it," Dr. Dave said. "She said the other girls gave her a piece of their minds. Maybe more than just a piece."

"That's what I thought," Jake said. "You don't mind if I follow you back there to talk to her? If she wants to leave town, I can escort her back to the campsite and make sure things don't get ugly between her and those other girls while she packs up. Might get her out of town faster that way."

"Sure," Dr. Dave said. He finished his drink, kissed Average and then wormed out the other side of the booth. Jake followed him to their parked cars.

Dr. Dave's house sat dark, empty and silent when he led Jake through the front door. The sheets where Jody slept still lay rumpled.

"No note," he said to Jake. "Typical."

"I'll have to check in with the dig and see if she went back there," Jake said.

Dr. Dave tucked his hands into his pockets. "Give it a few hours," he said. "Jody doesn't think in straight lines. If she's going to stay with *that* team, she may decide to buy them all doughnuts, follow up on research, or get her pouting done before she goes back. I bet she'll be there by noon."

"I could go back to the office and wait by the phone," Jake said. "With my luck, the State Medical Examiner's office might get to Scott's body soon."

Chapter 11

The old rotary phone in the Police Office rang when Jake walked in. He made it to the device by the sixth tone. In his haste to pick up the receiver, he fumbled it onto the desk.

"Tranquility P.D." He sat down as he lifted the earpiece to his ear.

"I'm calling the sticks, aren't I?" A growly female voice, like oil frying in the diner, droned on the other end of the line.

"Excuse me?" Jake asked.

"The sound quality on this line is superb: like a land phone. No one has a land line anymore unless they live in the Stone Age."

"That explains the dinosaur outside." Jake made a face. "This is Officer Coletrane, Who am I speaking to?"

"I'm Dr. Barnes with the State Medical Examiner's Office. How many people are in your town?" She sounded like the tourists who came to town every summer.

"About five hundred. What can I do for you, Dr. Barnes?"

"It's what I can do for you," she said. "For some reason the case you sent me got flagged as a priority. Normally we wouldn't move it up the queue just because of a computer glitch but I'm feeling generous. I performed a full autopsy on your victim yesterday."

"A computer glitch," Jake said. "Must be my lucky day."

"Must be," Dr. Barnes said. "I'll fax you my report when it's ready but I thought you might like preliminary findings. He drowned; make no mistake about that, officer. But someone helped your victim into the lake."

"I appreciate it," Jake said. "I knew the kid. He was a real nuisance but he didn't deserve to be killed. We had our local doctor consult before we sent the body to you. He's the one who thought it seemed odd."

"Your doctor has a good eye," Dr. Barnes said. "The head wound was angular like he hit his head on a brick, not a river stone. But there's more: next to the wound we found a bruise in the shape of an initial."

"Initial?" Jake asked.

"Some brick makers stamp their work before they fire the bricks. Could be that's what it's from."

"Could you send me a photo of the bruise?" Jake asked.

"I'll send it over right now," Dr. Barnes said. "Once we removed his clothes, we found a couple more bruises: one on the shoulder and one on the back. Your killer grabbed the victim from behind and held him in place while he or she hit the victim in the head, pushed him down and kicked him into the water."

"Can you tell anything about the killer from the bruises?"

"Based on the angle of the head wound, the killer was either really tall, or they stood uphill from the victim."

"That means that our victim faced the lake," Jake said. "Thanks, Dr. Barnes. I have a how. Now I just need a who."

"Good luck, Officer," Dr. Barnes said.

"I have all the luck I need," Jake replied before hanging up the phone. "I hope."

When Jake pulled up his email, he already had the message from Dr. Barnes. He clicked to open the attached photo and waited for the image to appear on his ancient computer.

The screen showed a grainy image of a mottled bruise. Dr. Barnes had traced the bruising with a marker to highlight a single letter, but Jake would have recognized it anyway. A reverse image of a stylized G inside a round coin shape with milling on the edges. The logo Rachel's Grampy Coin used for *The Gold Standard* resort.

Chapter 12

Rachel held the puppy in her lap, stroking its head with her right hand to reassure it. With her left hand, she brought a needle up to its posterior.

This won't hurt a bit, she told it.

Duke, her itinerant bald ferret supervised the process from a nearby table. *She's lying,* he cautioned.

What? the puppy yelped out. Before he could struggle away, she jabbed him with the needle and delivered the medicine.

There, she told the puppy. *It didn't hurt, did it? I startled you more than anything.*

The puppy gave her a hurt look as it wriggled away. Rachel let it down from her lap onto the floor. It curled into a ball and started to lick its bottom where she'd stuck it.

"Some help you were," she said in human to Duke. But the ferret already shifted his attention onto her keys where they dangled from a peg near the door.

Ooh look! A shiny! Get the shiny! I want the shiny!

Rachel made an exasperated sound. She pulled a piece of paper from her prescription pad, crumpled it and sent it bouncing past Duke's nose.

Mine! Duke took off after the ball of paper, releasing an excited "dooking" noise. He tackled it, then went skidding off the edge of the table. Rachel peered over the edge after him. Duke shook himself, then dragged the ball under a closet door, never to be seen again.

"I lose more sets of keys that way," Rachel said. Before she could get the puppy back into his crate, the door chimed as it opened and Jake came through the entrance.

"Be right there, Jake!" She said as she scooped the puppy up. "Just have to take care of this rascal."

"Winn's granddaughter finding new puppies for you to care for?" Jake asked. Last time, Winn's youngest granddaughter adopted a Boston Terrier. An ugly breed plagued with constant gas and continual snorting like a pig. This one's eyes fixed in two different directions. It tilted its head to one side or another in order to see, had teeth missing on one side of its mouth and a tongue hanging out on the same side as the missing teeth.

The girls named it Bella.

"Since the older girl claimed Bella, the younger one wanted this puppy," Rachel said. "At least this one seems smart. Bella makes Duke look like an Ivy League candidate." As she spoke, Duke stumbled across the waiting room floor with one of her sneakers caught on his head. She put the puppy into his crate and chased after the ferret to save him. As soon as she pulled the shoe from his head, he ran for the safety of her desk.

"What can I do for you?"

"You can start with a kiss." Jake grinned at her.

Rachel did so with a laugh. "It's not lunchtime, so this must be a business call. Is something wrong with the lake?"

"I need some more information on your Grampy's hotel." Jake explained the State Medical Examiner's findings. "Did your Grampy custom-make bricks that he used?"

"He sure did," Rachel said. "Right there when they built the resort. Momma said they put a brick maker's kiln on site."

"What did they use the bricks for?" Jake asked.

"Cobblestone pavers for the streets and bricks for the buildings. Every one with a *Gold Standard* stamp on it."

"Any idea who might have a brick from the old resort?"

"Have you tried eBay?" She tilted her head back.

Jake's heart sank. "I hoped most of them were still at the bottom of the lake," he said. "Whoever has one might be the killer."

"Sorry, hon." Rachel smoothed an imaginary wrinkle in his shirt. "When the resort opened, people used to steal them for souvenirs. Momma said Grampy hired a guard to search people's bags for stolen bricks. The good news is that there aren't a lot left in the area. So that narrows your list of suspects down, since I doubt a random collector from Alaska would fly down just to kill Scott with a brick."

"They might once they met Scott." Jake pinched the bridge of his nose.

"You could ask Mr. Moder," Rachel said. "He was trying to find anyone with memorabilia from the resort for his documentary."

"Good idea," he said. Then he had a new thought. "The Historical Society has the brick from your family collection, don't they? I could use it for reference—and make sure it's not bloody on one corner."

"I think so," Rachel said. "Mom gave them most of that junk."

Jake placed a smooch on Rachel's lips. "Thanks hon. Meet you at the diner for lunch?"

"See you there," Rachel said.

As soon as Jake left, Duke dive-bombed the sleeping clinic cat from the top of the bookshelves. *Banzai!* He screamed as he flew through the air.

The cat let out a startled scream and hiss when the ferret landed on him. *Get off of me you overgrown rat!*

"It's like working with an over-caffeinated two year old," Rachel said.

The Tranquility Historical Society didn't maintain a museum so much as a few glass cases in the hall of the gas station. Bob--who called himself "Lord Valentine" and participated in historical reenactment and wedding planning in his off hours--took care of them as president of the society. If anyone wanted to know the history of Tranquility, they talked to him while getting a fill-up or an oil change.

Once he'd planned Jake's wedding as "Lord Valentine," he never bothered dropping out of persona around Jake.

"Ah! Our town's foremost citizen! 'Ow can I 'elp you?" He asked in a fake French accent when Jake walked in the front door.

"I wanted to find out a little more about *The Gold Standard* memorabilia in your collection," Jake said.

Lord Valentine laid a finger alongside his nose. "Just so! I expected to hear from you when you found *les mortis cadaver.*"

Jake wrinkled his forehead as he puzzled through Lord Valentine's words. He suspected the faux Frenchman learned his French from Babelfish translations on the internet. "Between Rachel and Mr. Moder, I've got two good resources on

The Gold Standard already. I just want to see your brick from the resort."

Lord Valentine appeared hesitant. "Er. Si. I think ...Un Momento, Por Favor."

"That's Spanish," Jake said in a flat voice. "Did something happen to the brick?"

"Happen?" Lord Valentine let out an uncomfortable chuckle. "Not in so many words, non. La petite brick was just mislaid."

"You can't find it?"

"We cleaned the cases in preparation for the visit from Mr. Moder. When we put the items back, the brick was not among them."

Jake's right eye started to tic. "Who has access to those cases?"

Lord Valentine started to tick off the names of his retinue on his fingers. "Lord Doug, Antonia, Ze Duke of Earl, Lady Elane, Captain Morgan, Monk—"

"All of your Renaissance Wedding Planners," Jake cut in. "Anyone else?"

"Half ze town stopped in for service that morning," Lord Valentine said with a shrug.

Jake crossed his arms. "Someone could've used the brick in a murder," he said. "I need the *legal* name and the number of every one of your friends along with their alibi for when that boy drowned. And I need you to give me a list of everyone who stopped in when you cleaned those cases."

"Zat is a lot of people. 'Ow do I remember everyone?" Lord Valentine scratched his head.

"Credit card receipts may help with some of them. If all else fails, you can ask the other Historical Society members. Everyone should be nice and helpful, Lord Val. You're all going to need each other for alibis anyway."

Lord Valentine sighed with a put-upon huff. "Bien, officer."

Jake put on his sunglasses on the way back to the car. Before he could get behind the wheel, Marco's vehicle pulled past the pumps and up to the door. The professor got out and approached Jake's cruiser.

"Mornin'." Jake touched an imaginary hat in greeting. "Have you heard from Jody yet?"

"I got off the phone with her a half-hour ago," Marco said. "She's on her way home to Memphis. I think she got sick of trying to get along with the others in the department."

"I'm just glad I don't have to file a missing person's report. There's enough on my plate with the body we found in the lake."

"How is the investigation going?" Marco asked.

"I heard back from the State Medical Examiner today," Jake said. "The case just officially became a homicide. I'm going to have a couple of part-time security guards patrolling the area, but your crew should stick together. There's safety in numbers."

Marco seemed troubled. "I'll let Sandy and Maggie know," he said. "Good thing we're staying in the hotel now instead of camping."

"Sorry things didn't work out with your girlfriend," Jake said. The two men waved to each other and Marco walked away as Jake got in his cruiser and headed to his office.

To Jake's relief, Dr. Dave's Nova sat in front of town hall. Now he wouldn't have to track down the Doc to tell him about Jody.

Dr. Dave sat in the chair across from Jake's desk playing some kind of game on his phone.

Jake took a seat as the doctor put his phone away. "Good news, Doc. Professor Caseri said that Jody went home."

Dr. Dave scratched his head. "That's funny. I just called her parents in Memphis and they haven't heard from her since the day before she came to me in tears."

"Maybe she was so upset that she forgot to call them."

Dr. Dave shook his head. "Not Jody. She calls her parents every day when she's *happy*. When she's upset, it's like the phone is surgically attached to her ear."

Chapter 13

Jake opened his rolodex to the "M" and thumbed through it until he found Gerry "Geronimo" Moses. Then he dialed the number.

Gerry picked up after a few rings. "Lucky! I haven't heard from you since those murders at your wedding!"

"Hey, Geronimo." Jake grinned at the sound of his nickname from back at the academy. "How's business?"

"Not as slow as in that podunk town where you work. Are you ever going to join up with the state force?"

"Your boys couldn't afford me," Jake teased.

"Pull the other leg," Geronimo said. "What can I do for you?"

"I need to put an *Attempt to Locate* notice out."

"What's going on this time?" Geronimo's voice became serious.

Jake sketched out the conflict between Jody and her teammates, and her subsequent disappearance.

"You sure you should start an alert just yet?" Geronimo asked. "Sometimes these things end up being misunderstandings."

"I'm already working one murder up here," Jake said. "Someone killed a treasure hunter around the dig site."

"What does the girl look like?"

Jake described Jody and her habit of talking in questions.

"I'll get this out on the radio, Lucky. As for suspects, you know who to ask first."

Jake put his head in his hand. "Yeah, I know," he said. "Either the boyfriend or the ex. Problem is, the boyfriend was with his archaeology team all night. And the ex is our town doctor."

"Does the ex have an alibi? He's got a bigger motive."

"Half of one," Jake said.

"One half too few, if you ask me." Geronimo said. "Let me know if you need anything else."

"Will do." Jake hung up, feeling glum and leaned back in his chair to stare up at the ceiling. The facts of the case circled in his head in a demented ring-around-the-rosy. No matter what, he couldn't make them stand still.

He was about to go to the diner to find Average, when she walked into the office.

"Speak of the Devil." Jake sat up.

"Never been called that before." Average sat across from him. "What's wrong?"

"What time did Dr. Dave go to your house last night?"

Average's forehead creased in concern. "Just after midnight."

"Did you walk him home?"

"I did. Right after closing time at the diner."

Jake grunted in disappointment. That left three hours of Dr. Dave's time they couldn't account for. "Has Dr. Dave seemed hostile to Jody? Did his emotional state worry you?"

Average's hesitation said enough.

Jake rubbed his forehead, feeling a migraine start. "Tell me what's going on with the Doc. The sooner we figure this all out, the sooner we can clear him"

"It sounds bad."

"Out with it, Av."

Average nodded. "Dr. Dave experienced...hallucinations every time he saw Jody. He asked me the other day if she reminded me of Sharon Stone in *Basic Instinct*. He wouldn't have told me *that* if I didn't know to ask. He feels pretty homicidal whenever he's in the throes of a hallucination."

"How detailed do these hallucinations get?" Jake asked.

"They end with something happening to Jody. But it's never anything he does himself. It's always some random thing," she added.

"Give me an example."

"He said he dreamed that General Custer ate her once." Average held up her right hand and began ticking instances off on her fingers. "Once he said that a satellite fell on her and once part of his ceiling caved in."

"That just makes him sound nuts," Jake said. "I think I need Dr. Dave to come in for questioning and stick around until either Jody turns up or we can clear his name. That way no one can say I let a crazy suspect run loose." He hoped that Dr. Dave wasn't two bricks shy of a load. He also hoped he couldn't link the Doc to a murder investigation.

"I understand, Jake." Average stood up and crossed to the exit.

"Where are you going?" Jake wanted to be the one to explain things to Dr. Dave.

"If he's going to be a jailbird, I'm going to make him a box lunch. I hope he won't need many of them."

"Just don't bake a file into a cake," Jake said.

Tracy S. Morris

Chapter 14: Now

Open up! Up! Up! Up! Up! Duke danced on the counter next to Rachel's cash register. *You have hooman beans out the door waiting on you! You need to let them in!*

Rachel gave the ferret a curious look before she parted the blinds at her window. A line of people stretched from her front door out into the clinic's gravel lot.

What in Sam Hill? she said to the ferret in his own language.

You don't have a hill. Duke stopped his bouncing and tilted his head sideways in confusion. *You have a flat space for cars with lots of rocks. It's rough and no good for making tunnels.*

Rachel ignored him in lieu of cracking the door open. Mrs. Paulson stood on the other side.

"See! I told you she would see you all today!" She said as she bulled her way past Rachel and into the lobby. She walked behind the cash register, picked up Duke and sat him on a nearby bookshelf.

"Your husband arrested Dr. Dave for the disappearance of that weird girl. You know the one. She spoke in questions." Mrs. Paulson made a snapping motion with her fingers as if she couldn't remember Jody's name.

"Mrs. P? What?" Rachel waved to indicate all the people pushing past her into the old sitting room that she used for a waiting room. After everyone else sat down, Mrs. Fisher moved one of Rachel's mother's doilies from the arm of her dad's old recliner and sat there.

"Jody! That's it!" Mrs. P pointed at Rachel as if she'd just supplied an answer to a question.

"Jody," Rachel echoed.

"I used my precognition to see that the Doc wouldn't be free by this morning. Then I foresaw you caring for his patients today. So I took the liberty of booking them in to see you. I hope you don't mind—But I know you don't since you already told me you didn't."

"No," Rachel said in a faint voice as she tried to keep up with Mrs. Paulson's clairvoyant conversation. "I don't suppose I mind."

The receptionist leaned across the counter to pat her on the shoulder. "Don't worry Dear, Dr. Dave doesn't have a choice. So he will sign off on all your charts and Jimbo will fill the prescriptions. I've already seen it. And I haven't booked anyone else in for this afternoon, since I know you have plans.

"You know I'm not an M.D. So Dr. Dave wouldn't like me to see two-legged animals." Rachel fulfilled her duty by finishing her half of the conversation so Mrs. Paulson wouldn't become confused. "I have plans this afternoon," she added. "Thank you."

"You're welcome, Dear," Mrs. Paulson said at the exact same time. "Oh! I remembered to wait for you to finish your side of the conversation before starting mine!" She skipped in excitement. "I think? It sounded backward to me, so it must have been right."

"You did fine, Mrs. Paulson." Rachel waved for Debbie to follow her back into the exam room.

In the tiny room that served as the combined office for the mayor, police and utilities, Jake passed Dr. Dave a telephone and a list of names. "Here's everyone who was in and out of the gas station while Lord Valentine and his crew cleaned the cases of stuff from *The Gold Standard*. Anyone on this list could get to the memorabilia; which means they're all potential suspects in the Walters murder."

"What do I do with it?" Dr. Dave ruffled the papers in his hands.

"See if they have an alibi for the morning Scott disappeared. That should narrow down our suspects."

"*I* don't have an alibi for the part of that morning before Average showed up," Dr. Dave said.

"You didn't even know Scott," Jake said. "If we clear your name on his murder, we can poke holes in your involvement with Jody's disappearance, too. While you're doing that I'm going to question Lord Valentine and his group."

Dr. Dave glanced down at the list. Then he squinted at it harder. "Horace's name is on this list."

"He stopped into the gas station for a fill up. But I saw him at the diner when Scott Walters died," Jake said. "So take him off the list."

Dr. Dave pursed his lips in suspicion. He walked over to Horace's office, nudged it open and looked in. "Jake? You better see this."

With a sinking feeling, Jake got up and walked to the door. A yellow brick with a stylized G stamped into one side sat on top of Horace's desk. "Well crap."

"Yeah." Dr. Dave dragged the word out, his voice sounding like the diner's grease fryer. "He might've taken the Historical Society's brick to use as a paperweight."

"Since to Horace's way of thinking it's all city property anyway." Jake threw up his hands. "Which means that's probably not the brick used as a murder weapon. We'll have to test it, but I bet we're right back to square one!"

Chapter 15

When Rachel brought the vehicle to a halt at the lake's boat ramp, Tommy jumped out of the truck and grabbed a dip net. He charged full-tilt to the water's edge, where Michael Moder stood with a rubber raft.

Rachel reached for her thermos of juice, wishing for strong diner coffee instead. She hadn't expected to have a full day's work this morning when she opened the clinic. Her reflection in the rearview showed that tufts of hair had escaped from her pony tail and she sported dark circles under her eyes.

She reached into her glove box for concealer and a hair brush, but instead found empty tranquilizer darts, and Duke.

What are you doing in there? She asked in exasperation.

It's warm and cozy. Duke yawned and stretched. Rachel draped the ferret behind her neck like a living travel pillow. Then she raked her fingers through her hair to shove the wayward strands into place. "Remind me to get more concealer at the drug store tonight."

Does it taste good? Duke asked.

I doubt it, Rachel said. She walked down to meet Tommy and Mr. Moder.

"Do you plan to bring your step-son on this trip?" The director said in annoyance. Rachel ground her teeth. She'd had the exact conversation with Jake earlier that day.

Are you sure that's a good idea? Going in the boat in your condition? And taking Tommy? After what happened to the sonar?

"We're staying in the shallows," Rachel said.

"*That's not very reassuring.*"

"If there is a giant catfish, I'm sure I could reason with it," Rachel said. "It'll be fine."

Jake sighed. "Yes, Dear."

"He's part of the Coin family now." Rachel crossed her arms. "So he should be in your video. Besides, he wants to catch frogs and he won't ruin your camera the way that archaeology student did."

He flinched at the mention of the accident at the dig site. Then shook off the reaction and smiled down at Tommy in a saccharine way. "Are you going to be a good little boy today?"

Tommy gave him an unimpressed look. "Sure, Mister. Are you going to be condescending the whole trip?"

"That's a very big word," Michael said.

"I can spell it too. C-O-N-..."

"Okay, kid. I get it." He cut Tommy off.

Rachel hid a laugh behind her hand. "Let's get started, shall we?"

Tommy hopped into the boat, followed by Rachel. "Life jacket!" He told her.

"We're not going in very deep." Michael said.

Rachel put on the life vest, then tugged at the straps of Tommy's to make sure it was secure.

Michael rolled his eyes, pushed the boat away from the bank and then settled in the bow section. He turned on a camera and then put it on the seat next to him so it pointed at Rachel. Then he picked up an oar and rowed.

Water still submerged the buildings around the perimeter of the lake by about four feet. Rachel could see most of the lodge as well as the edge of the amphitheater seats. Further into the lake, the bank looked almost halfway uncovered and beyond that the first rooftops of farmhouses were visible.

"Grampy Coin would spin in his grave if he knew how much business this was bringing the hotel up the hill," she said. "Sarah tells me that they've filled every room. People are coming from miles around just to see these old buildings."

"Where did your family bury your grandfather?" Michael asked. "The records that I found said he rests under the lake somewhere."

Rachel laughed. "Oh no! We buried Grampy Coin in a family vault up the hill from here." She pointed to a thin spot in the trees a mile away from the *Hotel des Portiers*. "But don't put that in your documentary. We don't talk about it outside the family. Folk might break into his vault searching for treasure."

Michael followed her gaze. "I don't see anything," he said.

"The trees hide it," Tommy shot back.

"There's not much to see," Rachel said. "It's just a gray cement vault sticking out of the ground. Grampy only made it big enough for two coffins - his and his oldest son's. Grammy wanted to be buried in Tranquility cemetery with the rest of the family."

"How much trouble have treasure hunters been?" Michael asked.

"Folks started spreading the rumors right after Grampy died." Rachel said. "Grammy even opened the vault for reporters about five years after he passed. They went over it with a fine-toothed comb. Only found the two coffins."

"Where did all his money go?" Tommy asked.

"Momma said he once sent a good chunk of cash to a group of industrialists in Germany to help them build something called a *tepaphone*," Rachel rolled the word around in her mouth to make the pronunciation more precise. "They said it would amplify telepathic powers from a distance. But he stopped funding them when he found out they wanted it so they could kill people with their minds. Grammy said that he did stuff like that all the time. Usually she cursed when she said it."

"Is that where you came up with the idea of a swear jar?" Tommy asked.

Rachel laughed. "I near-funded my college education on the swear jar."

Michael passed Tommy the oar and picked up the video camera to film. Based on his expression, Rachel figured he was trying to keep Tommy busy and out of the way. They steered away from the ruins of the bank, toward the old lodge.

Tommy leaned from one side of the boat to the other, making it rock and sending waves out from the sides. Michael shot him a dirty look

"Relax, Mr. Moder," Rachel said with an indulgent smile. "Tommy only weighs 65 pounds. I doubt he'll tip your raft."

Tommy's pole hit something on the bottom of the lake near the amphitheater with a metal thud. Pockets of stale-smelling air erupted from the water with a muddy, flatulent sound, rocking the boat. The three of them grasped the rubber sides of the craft as it drifted away from a set of expanding ripples.

"See!" Rachel said once she found her voice again. "It's stable."

"What happened?" Tommy asked.

At the center of the ripples, leaf-like debris appeared.

"Look!" Rachel picked up Tommy's dropped oar and brought the boat around again.

"Don't strain yourself!" Michael said.

Rachel snorted in derision. "I'm pregnant, not an invalid." Most of the floating debris looked like some kind of paper. She picked up one of the sodden sheets, held it up to the light and recognized the spidery handwriting from the family bible. "This was Grampy's!" She said. "I think we might've hit the time capsule!" She threw the sodden paper down into the floor of the boat and reached for another. "Tommy! Get the frog net!"

The boy grabbed the net and started scooping papers into the boat.

"I wonder what else we might find down there?" Michael asked as he filmed the two of them while they worked at a feverish pace.

"I'm sure Grampy wrote about whatever it is in here." Rachel waved a page in the air to flick water off of it. "Put your camera down and help us, otherwise we'll never get them all!"

Michael sat the camera in the seat next to him and started grabbing pages.

Rachel squeezed into Jake's office between The Duke of Earl and Monk, the Viking babysitter. The members of the Historical Society perched in every available spot. Lord Valentine jumped out of his seat to offer it. Not to be outdone, Captain Morgan also leaped up. Before she could sit Monk pushed his chair into the backs of her knees. Rachel plopped into the seat with an ungraceful grunt.

Dr. Dave sat in the new jail cell in the corner. He gave her a cheerful wave. Rachel waved back.

"Why are you sitting there?" she asked him.

"No room anywhere else." Dr. Dave pushed on the cell door to show he could get out.

"How come you guys aren't at the gas station?" she asked Lord Valentine, the group's erstwhile leader.

"We're clearing our good name." Lord Valentine pressed the back of his hand to his forehead in a near swoon. "Les gendarme suspects us in a recent murder." He reclined on a bench against a wall and held a lace handkerchief to under his nose. "I feel faint! My condition is quite delicate, you know."

Tommy raced into the room. He took in the Historical Society members in their full medieval regalia and clapped his hands in delight. "Mr. Monk! Did you bring your foam swords?"

"They're out in the car," Monk pointed at the parking lot. "You'll have to ask your step-mom if it's okay to go play with them.

"It's fine." Rachel glanced around the room. "Where's Jake?"

"Running down a lead." Dr. Dave tilted his head in the direction of Horace's office. "He'll come out here in a minute."

Tommy cheered and pulled the wannabe Viking from the room just as Jake exited the mayor's office, holding a yellow brick in the air.

"Anyone recognize this?" He turned it so Rachel could see the stamp with the large G in it.

"That's a family brick," she said. "Where did you find it?"

Jake put the brick on his desk and tucked his hands in his pockets. "Let's just say that a citizen liberated it from the Historical Society's collection to use as a paperweight."

"Zen' we are—'ow do you say, in the clear?" Lord Valentine sat up.

"You're all free to go. Take this brick with you," Jake said to Lord Valentine.

"How do you know it's not the murder weapon?" Rachel asked.

"There isn't any blood on it," Jake said.

"Good," Rachel said. "Because I may have a job for this group, if you aren't going to lock them up."

"Indeed?" Lord Valentine lifted an eyebrow. "What sort of task?"

"Can you restore documents?" She held out a sodden sheet of paper.

Lord Valentine took the paper from her hands. "What is 'zis?"

"Tommy and I found the time capsule," Rachel said.

"Quite by accident, from the condition of things," Lord Valentine placed the wet paper on the corner of Jake's desk. "These appear to be ledgers."

"Bookkeeping records," Rachel said. "If there's anything else hidden on the property, it's recorded somewhere in these papers. But I need someone who can preserve them before they deteriorate anymore."

"Leave 'zat to us!" Lord Valentine handed the flattened paper to The Duke of Earl. "Do you have more?"

"I took all my tools out of my truck box, but the old diaries and ledgers plum filled it up."

Lord Valentine looked horrified. "You put them in a common tool box? Why not just give them to your ermine friend to chew on?"

From his spot on Rachel's shoulder, Duke made an angry noise.

"Do you want the documents or not?" Rachel stroked the ferret to calm it.

Lord Valentine held up his hands. "Be at peace, tiny creature. I meant no disrespect." With a final huffy chitter, Duke tucked his head into the pocket of Rachel's shirt. One by one, the Historical Society members filed out of the office. As Jake stood to follow them, his phone rang.

Rachel paused by the door and watched Jake pick up the phone. His expression darkened at whatever he heard.

"What's wrong?" She asked when he hung up.

"Billy called. Emmet spotted another body in the lake."

Chapter 16

Once again, Rachel found herself standing at the top of the boat ramp overlooking the lake. A body floated head-down in the water, meters from the ruins of the old bank. It was tangled in some brush, which kept it from sinking despite the rocks tied to it.

It wasn't Jody—hair color and body shape were wrong. So that meant *maybe* three people were dead.

That marked the second time they lucked into a crime scene. If she could call what Jake had "luck." Some days Rachel wondered.

"We just came from here." The thought sent a shiver up her spine. "Someone either came along to dump the body after we left, or was here watching us the whole time."

"Bet that's why the killer dumped the body so fast," Jake said. "They worried about being spotted."

Rachel turned to watch Dr. Dave, Billy and Emmet unload the Johnboat. "Do you plan to keep holding the Doc over Jody?" she asked.

"Not unless her parents file a missing person's report," Jake said. "Anyway, we need him to consult in this murder."

Dr. Dave and the two security guards dropped the lightweight boat into the water with a splash.

"Should I go with you this time?" Rachel asked.

"No," Jake said. "Just stay here with Billy and Emmet and keep an eye out for anything suspicious. Do you have your tranquilizer gun in the truck?"

Rachel nodded. "Do you need me to keep The Two Stooges in line?"

"No, but if you see anyone lurking around, shoot 'em just in case."

"We're going to have a panic if this body is some random tourist," Rachel said.

Jake grunted in agreement. Held the boat steady while Dr. Dave got in. Then he jumped in behind the Doc.

"The State M.E. said that the killer grabbed Scott by the shoulder and hit him from behind with a brick," Jake said. "Then pushed him into the water."

"I should at least be able to give you an indication whether the cause of death is the same," Dr. Dave said.

As Jake pushed the boat up to the body with a pole, Dr. Dave gasped. "Jake, I think that's one of the archaeologists. The tall one..." He trailed off, snapping his fingers. Then he pointed at Jake. "Sandy!"

Jake's heart sped up. The old resort and its treasure sat at the center of all of this somehow. But did that make Jody another victim? Or a killer laying low?

Jake put aside his musing to focus on the body in front of him. He picked up his camera and handed it to Dr. Dave. The Doc photographed the body from several angles as Jake pushed the boat around it. Then the two of them spread a tarp in the floor of the craft just as they did with Scott and lifted the corpse on top of it. While Jake slipped plastic bags over the hands, Dr. Dave put on a pair of blue rubber gloves and examined her mouth.

"She didn't drown," he said. "There's no foam in her airway like with the other body. And she went through the early stages of rigor before she went into the water." He tilted her head to the side, revealing a wound behind her ear.

"A brick could've done this. There is very angular bruising. Also, see the crusted blood? Scott had a clean wound. I think our killer bludgeoned her."

"Whoever murdered Scott Walters did it on the fly," Jake said. "But the killer planned this one." He picked up his phone and called Average.

"Hi, Jake." Average sounded like she was at the mayor's office instead of the diner. "Dr. Dave isn't in the jail. Did you release him?"

"Just now. We're working a new murder," Jake said.

"Oh, no!"

"Average, can you do me a favor?"

"Sure?" Her voice rose in cautious question.

"Can you call Scott Walters' family? I should have their numbers in his case file. Ask them if he had a *Gold Standard* brick. If so: have them check if it's missing."

"Okay, Jake," she said. "I'll try to have the information by the time you get back."

"Thanks!" Jake hung up. Off Dr. Dave's querulous expression, he explained. "I think the killer may have encountered Scott Walters up at the lake. Scott had some theory about subterranean caves where Old Man Coin used to hide his treasure."

Jake knelt in the boat and continued to talk as he and Dr. Dave wrapped up the body in the tarp. "Maybe our killer thought the same thing and he didn't want anyone else taking the treasure first. Our killer is a fellow collector and he or she has a brick. Or maybe Scott has a brick and the killer asks to see it. Either way, Scott trusts him enough to turn his back. And the killer uses the brick to knock Scott in the head."

"Then Sandy does something to make the killer uneasy," Dr. Dave said.

"Sandy was a member of the Corps of Engineers," Jake said. "They're the ones who built the original lake. Maybe she found something in the original studies or records and the killer got nervous enough to eliminate her."

They secured the tarp with ties and then Jake took up his pole again. On the shore, Winn's truck and an ambulance pulled up to the boat dock. "I'm going up to the archaeologists' camp to let them know what happened."

"Better take backup," Dr. Dave said. "Make it Rachel, not Billy or Emmet. She's a better shot and one of the remaining archaeologists might be the killer."

Jake grunted in acknowledgement. "It won't be the first time I've deputized her. Or even the hundredth."

The archaeologists' camp looked abandoned as Jake and Rachel pulled up. Jake squinted in suspicion at the empty tents. "Think they're all up at the hotel?"

"Maybe they're up there avoiding the smell," she said. They followed the winding road up the hillside to the *Hotel des Portiers*. As they entered the ornate lobby, Sarah sat up from behind the front desk.

"Jake? Have you seen Billy?"

"He's down at the lake with Emmet," Jake said. "There's been another murder."

Sarah groaned and hid her face in her hands. "Just send him back up here as soon as you can spare him," she said. "The guests will feel safer if there is a visible guard on the premises."

"Sarah, are the archaeologists from the dig still here in the hotel?"

Sarah pointed up to the second story balcony. "I think I saw the guy in charge go into the coffee bar."

"Thanks," Jake said as they left.

He and Rachel found Marco sitting at a table studying a map of *The Gold Standard* with a perturbed expression on his face.

"Professor Casari?" Jake asked to get his attention.

Marco waved in greeting. "What can I do for you today?"

"We just came from your camp. Where did everyone go?" Jake asked.

"Not much point in being down there today," Marco said. "My team is gone."

"Gone?" Jake asked.

"Both Sandy and Maggie packed up last night," Marco said. "They told me some very unkind things before they left. I'm waiting for a couple of new volunteers to come help me finish the dig."

Jake and Rachel shared a concerned look. "Can we see the room you guys rented?" he asked.

"Sure." Marco rose from his chair. "What's this about?"

"I have some bad news," Jake said. "We found Miss Dupree in the lake not long ago."

Marco gulped. "*In* the lake?" He turned to Rachel. "What about Maggie?"

"We hoped we'd find her here with you," Jake said. Marco's head whipped around to Jake. "Her absence is more than a little suspicious."

"But Sandy and Maggie went everywhere together!" Marco fisted his hands in his hair. "They were partners! Like Butch and Sundance, Batman and Robin, Rocky and Bullwinkle, Sid and Nancy."

"Didn't Sid kill Nancy?" Rachel asked.

"My point is: if Sandy is dead then Maggie must be in some kind of trouble!" Marco said.

"We'll look into Maggie's disappearance." Jake cut Marco off to calm him. "But we need to see your rooms."

Marco gulped down his coffee and led them up to a fourth floor suite. For their wedding last summer, Jake and Rachel had booked a penthouse suite on the uppermost floor. The suite the archaeologists shared was about a quarter of that size. It consisted of a bedroom with a balcony and a sitting room with a fold-out sofa, desk and television set.

"Maggie and Sandy slept in this room. I took the bedroom." Marco waved around.

"What about Jody?" Rachel asked.

"Jody shared the bedroom with me," Marco said. A bitter smile crossed his face. "She never could keep a secret, so everyone knew of our relationship. No point in keeping up appearances."

"How do your superiors feel about that?" Rachel asked.

"I don't expect it will reflect well on my reviews when I come up for tenure," Marco said. "But I understand that her fiancée had a promising career in medicine before getting engaged to her. She seems to lay waste to men the same way Godzilla lays waste to small fishing villages."

Jake looked around the room while Rachel and Marco talked. A set of maps and papers formed a tower on the coffee table in front of the television. The pillows on the sofa lay askew and the refrigerator hung open. Most of the complimentary food and drinks were gone. The ones left were open and half-eaten. In the bathroom, towels lay crumpled on the floor. One wash cloth with makeup stains on it dangled from the towel rack. An empty, zippered bag lay on the counter.

By contrast, Marco's room looked immaculate. The professor had pushed his bed covers back into place to look like it'd been made. His clothing hung in his closet and his suitcase stood open on a rack at the foot of his bed. Other than a single hair tie, no evidence remained of Jody's exodus.

"Where do you keep most of your tools and supplies?" Jake asked.

"We've got them locked up in our van down in the parking lot," Marco said. "There isn't room up here and we aren't dumb enough to leave them at the campsite where someone could steal them."

There weren't any clues. If each girl left of her own free will, she'd done a thorough job packing. And if someone made them leave, they'd scoured the room afterward.

"Thank you, Professor Casari," Jake said. "Keep in touch."

Chapter 17

Jake leaned against the window next to his seat in Rachel's truck so he could see her better. "I've got three theories. One: Jody killed Scott, Sandy and Maggie and went on the lam to find your Grampy's treasure."

"If that's true, then she deserves an academy award for her bubble-brain act," Rachel said. "What are your other theories?"

"Two: Maggie killed Scott, Sandy and Jody for the same reason. Or three: Marco killed them all."

"You're overlooking a fourth possibility." Rachel held up four fingers. "One or more of those people could be in cahoots with the others."

"There's one thing to do: beat the killer to the spot where they think your Grampy's treasure is. Then we set a trap and wait for them to come to us."

"Then we're going to need information from Lord Valentine and Michael. If we hurry, we can catch them at the gas station." Rachel put her truck into drive.

An incessant knocking cut into Alice's nap. She looked up in time to see Winn peering in at her from her large bay window. She jumped in shock. Then she picked up a knitting needle and held it like a weapon. "Winthrop Stevens! You better have a good excuse for peeping in on me!"

She opened the door to find Horace standing there, hat in hand. "Alice, is Rachel here?" He asked.

Alice put her hands on her hips. "She's at work. What's going on?"

"It's General Custer!" Jimbo stepped out from her bushes to stand next to Horace. Winn came to stand behind the other two. All three men looked a sorry sight.

"Can you call her?" Winn put his hand together in prayer. "We found the General high and dry in the ruins of the old resort. If we don't act fast, he'll suffocate! We need Rachel to haul her stock tank over and save him!"

Alice reached for her phone, then thought better of it. She lifted her chin. "I'll call Rachel on one condition."

"Anything!" Horace said.

"You stop this stupid idea of courting me!" She waved a finger at Winn.

"Anything but that!" Winn gasped.

"I mean it, Winthrop Stevens! No more clumsy attempts at asking me out on a date!"

Winn chewed his lip as he looked from Horace to Jimbo. Jimbo held his hand out to Winn in a beseeching manner while Horace made shooing motions. Winn put a hand over his eyes. "Alright! I'll stop!"

"Good." Alice picked up the phone and dialed Rachel's number.

"Rachel hung up her phone, threw it on her dashboard and gave Jake a whimsical smile. "What do you know about that?"

"What happened?" Jake asked.

"Those crazy old fishermen found General Custer. We need to make a slight detour, Jake. They're asking me to rescue that old fish for them."

"They want us to stage a rescue while you're in...?" Jake trailed off, gesturing at her stomach. "I thought they wanted to taxidermy him."

"Some things are just too majestic to let die," Rachel said. "I guess that includes a giant, man-eating catfish. If we hurry, we can rescue it and still get to the gas station before Michael leaves town. And don't worry about me and the baby, you can do all the heavy lifting." She switched her truck into four wheel drive and rolled over the muddy lake bed until they reached the ruins of the old hotel.

"Very generous of you," Jake said.

"What was that?" Rachel got out of the truck and stared at him across the hood, eyes narrowed in challenge.

"Nothing, Dear."

"There isn't time to get the stock tank. We're going to have to improvise." Rachel produced a tarp from her tool box and used it to line her truck bed. Then she pulled out a garden hose and ran one end into the lake. She siphoned brackish water into the bed, forming a makeshift swimming pool. Then she scanned the shoreline until she spotted Billy and Emmet.

"We can use your jacket as a carry-sling and put General Custer into this temporary habitat. Once we get him home, I'll put him into my tank." Rachel waved Jake's temporary deputies over. Then she waded into the shallow water.

"How is this, my life?" With a chuckle of disbelief, Jake followed Rachel into the old hotel. They found the eight-foot-long fish trapped in a claw-footed bathtub. Rachel grabbed its lower lip between her thumb and forefinger. "That should keep it from thrashing and knocking us over," she said.

Just then Billy and Emmet waded into the room.

"What's up, Jake?" Billy asked.

Emmet caught sight of the fish. He nudged Billy and pointed out General Custer.

Billy gasped. "Holy Mackerel!" He let out a long whistle.

"Close," Rachel said. Then she slid her jacket under General Custer's head and fins. Jake put his coat around the big fish's tail. The two of them moved out of the way to let Billy and Emmet pick up the General and carry him to her truck. As they plopped the fish into the bed, Rachel saw the three old fishermen standing on the dock with their hats doffed.

Rachel cupped her hands around her mouth to yell. "He's alive. You guys can come by and pay your respects once I get him in a better tank."

"We're mourning the passing of Winn's love life!" Horace shouted back.

Rachel's jaw hung open.

"I'm sure we don't want to know," Jake said.

"We just got that monster fish taken care of. What now?" Jake pointed to the gas station.

Michael and Karl were loading equipment into a van with a History Channel logo on the side. Rachel and Jake exchanged glances and shrugged. She pulled in next to the van, honked the horn to get Michael's attention and leaned out her window. "What's going on?"

Michael's shoulders slumped. "I just got a call from Professor Casari. He called off the dig. He said He's already on his way back to Fayetteville."

Jake rolled down his window and leaned out. "What? We just spoke with him."

"It's true," Karl said as he wound a cable around a spool. "He said the University cut his funding. Someone's killing people who are interested in the lake and he can't get any more volunteers."

"I just don't get why." Michael held his hands up. "The professor seemed committed to the dig. He almost knew more about *The Gold Standard* than you did, Mrs. Coletrane."

A thought occurred to Jake. "Did the professor have a *Gold Standard* Brick?"

Michael's forehead wrinkled as he thought. "I'm not sure. But he let me film all his memorabilia. You can look at it, if you want." He motioned Jake into his van.

Inside the vehicle Michael plugged in a TV and cued up his video. Jake leaned in to better watch the screen as the footage played over a hodgepodge of *Gold Standard* items: ash trays, dinnerware, post cards and a rectangular, yellow brick.

"There!" Jake pointed at the screen. Michael paused the video on the image. Now that Jake could see the brick better, he spotted a dark stain on one corner. "I'll bet my luck that's blood," Jake said.

Rachel knocked on the door of the van. "Lord Valentine said that Average made some headway with the paperwork."

Jake climbed out of the vehicle and followed Rachel into the gas station. Old Man Coin's documents stretched out, drying over every available surface. In the center of it all, Average and Dr. Dave stood looking at the paperwork.

"Hi, Jake!" Average waved to him. "I called Scott Walters' family. They said Scott used to have a brick, but they thought he sold it to a professor at the University."

"Bingo." Jake hissed through his teeth. "Now we just need to find the treasure."

"There's nothing to find." Average pointed to the papers in front of her. "I don't see how Old Man Coin stayed in business as long as he did. He hemorrhaged money. Anything he didn't spend on his resort, he donated to fund bogus pseudoscience experiments." She held up a page and squinted at it. "I don't even know what a Multiple Wave Oscillator is."

"It was supposed to cure cancer by adjusting the oscillation of cells," Dr. Dave said. "No one took it seriously, though."

"I can see why not." Average laughed. "It sounds like something made up for a TV medical drama."

"Sounds like something my Grampy would have bought into," Rachel said. "Do those records say anything about storage? Something an archaeologist would think might be a hidden cache?"

Average pushed aside one of the crinkled sheaves of paper and held up a thin onionskin. "This says he spent several thousand dollars enlarging a system of caves in the side of the mountain and then lining them with clay waterproofing."

"Caves? What...Grampy's burial vault!" Rachel snapped her fingers. "It's the one bit of land he owned that wasn't in the valley." She pulled Jake toward the exit. "We've got to get my key to the vault!"

"Let's take my patrol car," Jake said. "Dr. Dave, why don't you and Average come, too?"

The four of them ran from the room.

Tracy S. Morris

Chapter 18

Jake pulled off the road leading up to the *Hotel des Portiers* onto a weed-choked side-path that went to the Coin family burial vault. Between a sprinkle of rain, the close-growing canopy and the encroaching underbrush, little light filtered through. The police cruiser bobbed over the ruts like a ship at sea.

"Someone's come this way before us," Rachel said as she leaned out the window. "The weeds in the ruts are crushed down."

"Then we're on the right track," Jake said.

"How do you know it's not just some kids?" Dr. Dave asked.

"Most of the kids go to Fort Smith to hang out," Jake said. "Unless they're off-roading. And those are definitely not quad tracks."

The path widened just before entering a clearing. Jake blinked in the sudden brightness. Before him, uncut spring-green grass grew knee-high. The tracks led to the mausoleum, then doubled back. In the distance, thunder rumbled.

Jake swore. "Missed 'em."

Rachel slumped in the seat next to him. "Oh well, at least we can look around."

At the vault door, Rachel produced her key and tilted the antique iron padlock up. "Yup, fresh scratch marks. Someone picked the lock," she said.

"Don't touch anything else. We'll dust for prints before we go." Jake put a hand on Rachel's arm. "Average, why don't you stand lookout? You sense anything with your empathy, give us a holler."

"Will do, Jake." Average stationed herself in a crouch where the tall grass would hide her.

The door groaned on rusty hinges as Rachel pulled it open. The smell of stale air and dust drifted over them.

115

"Hello? Marco?" Jody's faint, hoarse, desperate voice called out from inside the crypt.

"Behold: the sound of evil," Dr. Dave said.

Jake held his finger to his lips. Jody sounded like she might be in trouble, but she also might be a killer.

"Did you bring your tranquilizer gun?" Jake whispered as he pulled out his police-issue taser.

Rachel held up a tranq pistol. "I'm glad we bought this," she whispered back. "It's more convenient than the rifle."

Jake pulled out his light. Then, the four of them filed into the crypt. Recent footprints covered the dusty cement floor. Plaster hung from three of the walls. The fourth had crumbled, revealing a deeper cave.

Rachel reached out to touch the crumbling plaster. "It's soaked."

"Condensation," Jake said. "Should be safe enough to squeeze in."

At some point, Rachel's grandfather had cut stone shelves into the cave walls across from the plaster false wall. As Jake's light played over each shelf, the beam caught the muted glow of tarnished brass, moldy, untreated leather and warped wood.

"Is that a Tesla coil?" Dr. Dave asked. "This is like a Victorian scrap yard."

"Marco? This isn't funny? I'm hungry, and I'm cold?" Jody's voice rose in a plaintive wail.

"She sounds scared, Jake," Rachel said. "I don't think she's making it up."

He jerked his head in acquiescence, then called out. "Jody? It's Officer Coltrane. Yell so we can find you."

"Oh, thank goodness?" Jody sounded relieved. "I fell into a deep well and Marco went to get help?"

"When?" Jake asked.

"The other morning?" Jody said.

"No way she's a criminal mastermind." Rachel rolled her eyes.

"Hang on a second, Jody," Jake said. "We're going to get you some help!" He tossed Dr. Dave his keys. "I've got some rope in the trunk of my car. Get it so we can lower you down to reach her. And get on the horn to Central E.M.S. to get an ambulance on standby. She seems fine, but we might want a stretcher and a board to strap her to in case she's got some injury."

"Immobilizing her," Dr. Dave muttered as he left. "That'll just make her talk more."

Rachel set her jaw and lifted her gun higher. "How do you want to do this?"

"We need to find Professor Casari," Jake said. "I'll have a BOLO issued for him when we get back to town. Right now, Jody's our first priority."

Just then Dr. Dave and Average returned. The Doc had a thick coil of nylon rope slung over one shoulder and both of them held their hands in the air. Marco and Maggie walked behind them. Marco held a gun in the middle of Average's back.

"They were here all along!" Average cried.

"Sheriff, don't make me shoot her," Marco warned. "Drop your weapons."

Jake cursed as he held the taser up and placed it on the ground. Rachel followed with her tranq gun.

"How did you keep Average from sensing you?" Jake asked.

"They stayed out of my range." She shook her head with a rueful expression on her face. "By the time I spotted them, he already had his gun out."

"Now," Marco gestured to the wall where the plaster crumbled away. "I'm curious where Mrs. Coletrane thinks her Grandfather hid his treasure."

Average moved to stand with Dr. Dave and the four of them crawled through the rubble of the crumbled wall to the cave on the other side.

Rachel chuckled mirthlessly.

"What's so funny?" Marco sneered as he climbed through the hole.

"This," her wave took in the walls around her. "My Grampy gave his money to bogus science experiments. These are prototypes of their work. He believed in them enough to save them for future generations. Here's the treasure that you've killed for."

Marco's gun barrel shook and his face turned red.

"This junk?" Maggie whined. "It doesn't even have much intrinsic value in this condition."

"We could always try eBay." Marco took a deep breath. He gestured with the gun for them to keep moving. "I bet an old phrenologist's psychograph has antique value to the right collector. And you..." He turned the gun barrel back on Average. "No humming. I've been around your diner long enough to know about that head trick of yours."

The cave narrowed to a passage. At the end of it, a deep well opened up.

"Why is there a well in a mausoleum?" Dr. Dave asked.

"It existed before Mr. Coin bought it," Marco answered for them. "We found an old Civil War diary hidden in the University library. It described how Confederates put caches of weaponry in here. The water table sat lower then, before the lake changed everything. They dynamited an old spring to make a water well. After the war, bandits hid out in here. What better place for Old Man Coin to stash his goods?"

"Marco? You came back?" Jody sounded hopeful..

"It's also a good place to put people when you want to forget about them," Marco smirked.

Jake clenched his fist, if he hit Marco, Rachel might be able to get away with the baby. He might get shot, but at least she'd get away. Average grabbed his arm and shook her head.

Jake sighed. Maybe instead, if he could sow some dissent between Marco and Maggie, he and the others could overpower them while they were distracted.

He raised an eyebrow at Average. She nodded in silent agreement to that plan.

"We know you killed Scott Walters," Jake said. "I saw the weapon with blood on it in your stuff."

Maggie took a step away from Marco and looked at him in alarm. "I thought that was an accident?"

"I should have used a rock," Marco said. "The brick gave me away."

"What I don't understand is why you killed Miss Dupree," Jake pressed. "Was she going to reveal everything, too?"

Maggie paled. "You told me you sent Sandy back to Fayetteville for more supplies!"

Marco huffed in annoyance, then trained the gun on Maggie. "She outlived her usefulness, Maggie. Now you have too."

Maggie stared at him with her angry bluebird expression. She raised her hands and stepped over to the group in front of the pit.

"What's going on up there?" Jody asked. "Are you guys going to pull me out, or what?"

"Sandy told me that a bunch of water pooled in Coin's sealed caves after they built the lake. Now that the seals are failing, the water has nowhere to go but this crypt. It's going to flood before long." Marco said. "But I think by the time that happens, I'll be long gone with whatever I can take. Now drop the rope on the ground and all of you get in the well." He briefly pointed the barrel of the gun at the well.

Jake stepped to the edge of the well. "Jody? Stand back." He slid over the side and hoped his luck would hold.

The sides of the well sloped so that instead of falling, he rolled down into the bottom in a shower of rocks and dirt. The others tumbled after him.

Jake started toward Rachel, but Dr. Dave waved him off. He pulled out his light and looked around.

The bottom of the well widened into a cavern. Against one wall lay several long empty wooden crates stamped with the Confederate stars and bars. A pool of water sat to one side of the cave. A slow dripping sound filled the air.

Jody leaned against a rock wall, her arms crossed and her face smeared with dirt and tear tracks. "What are you doing here?" she asked. "I thought you were going to rescue me?"

"We're all in need of rescue, dummy!" Maggie snapped. "Your boyfriend sold us up the river!"

"Oh?" Jody trailed off.

"It gets worse," Maggie said to Jake. "Look at the water leaking through the walls. Sandy called it: this well sits lower than the caves with the trapped water in them. They're all lined with clay to keep water out, but the seal is crumbling. Pretty soon this whole thing is going to flood."

"I have more bad news!" Dr. Dave said.

Jake looked back at the Doc in fear. Were Rachel and the baby hurt?

"The fall caused my water to break," Rachel said through gritted teeth. "I'm in labor!"

119

Chapter 19

Jake played his light over the walls of the cavern, trying to ignore the growing pool in the corner. Over by the well opening, Dr. Dave had Rachel lay on her back to slow her contractions.

"David, you have to believe me? If I thought Marco was homicidal, I never would have given him that diary when I found it?" Jody wrung her hands.

"If you hadn't been so eager to impress lover boy here with how smart you are, Professor Caseri might not have shoved you down a well," Maggie muttered.

"Seriously?" Rachel groaned, her mouth set in a grim line. "Everyone who isn't in labor at the bottom of a freaking well, under a friggin' mountain—just shut up!"

Dr. Dave glared at Jody. "Later," he promised.

Jake cursed under his breath. There must be some way out that he just wasn't seeing. His luck hadn't failed him. Yet.

"Things look bad," Average murmured as she walked up next to him. "I know this is a crypt but I don't want to die."

"You're not going to," Jake said with confidence he didn't feel. "We just need to figure out what we got that can help us." He had a belt knife and a badge. Maybe he could gouge a ladder out of the dirt and scale the wall? Beyond that, what else might he have on hand?

Jake knelt over the discarded crates to get a better look. The wood seemed like new, not rotten like he would have expected from being inside an old well. The seams were still caulked. He bet the crates were waterproof.

In one, he found an old Sharps carbine with a pristine barrel and a broken stock. The soldiers who used them must have thrown them down here to get rid of them. The fact that they weren't in pieces proved that they were sturdy.

"I think these old crates might float like a boat," Jake said.

"What?" Maggie shrieked. "You're crazy! That won't work!"

"Why not?" Jake asked. "Two people can use one like a canoe. We steady them to keep from tipping and the water will lift us right up to the top of the well." He picked up the Sharps carbine.

Maggie put a hand on her hip. "You know what the odds are of this actually working?" She snapped.

Average shrugged. "It's Jake. The odds don't count with him."

"Besides, you haven't got a better idea?" Jody said.

"Out of the mouths of babes," Jake said.

He jerked his head up as the dripping sound from the walls increased to a trickle, then the gurgle of a fast stream. In moments the pool seemed to triple in size, sliding like hot molasses toward their feet. Whatever waterproofing Grampy Coin put in the well had just failed.

"No arguing! Everyone in!" He ordered. Average jumped in behind him. Dr. Dave helped Rachel climb into one and recline against him while Jody sat in another and waved for Maggie to join her. Maggie scoffed and climbed into a separate crate.

The water lifted Jake and Average's makeshift watercraft and sent it careening toward the wall. Jake used the barrel of the Sharps to steady the carton. Empty containers bumped and pushed like bumper cars at a county fair. Jake turned the rifle like a paddle and pushed the other boxes away from his own.

"If you tip over, try to hold onto the wood."

The water inched higher, carrying the crates like cars on the upward track of a roller coaster.

"This is not how I anticipated spending this dig." Maggie shoved her container away from Jake's.

"Becoming an accomplice to murder?"

"I had nothing to do with that," Maggie said. "We were just going to dig up some gold and bank it. If I get out of this –"

"*When* we get out of this, you're going to testify against Professor Caseri." Jake leaned away from Jody and put his hand to the side of his mouth to whisper. "You'd be a better witness."

"Because I don't have tapioca for brains?" Maggie snarled. "He killed Sandy. You bet your shorts I'll testify against him!"

"Jake," Average yelled, pointing over the side of the crate. "The water is running too fast to stop when we reach the top."

Jake looked at the sides of the well in alarm. The water pushed them all up like an express elevator. Soon it would hit the lip and follow the path of least resistance down the hill toward the mausoleum entrance.

"Hold on!" Jake called to the others. Then he shot through the smooth cavern as if riding a giant log flume.

Light up ahead signified the exit.

"Everyone duck!" Jake crouched below the lip of the crate. The edges of the wood above his head splintered as the craft shot through the opening like a torpedo.

Trees flashed past them in a blur. The tidal wave rolled down the hillside and before Jake knew it, he and Average were floating in the shallow water at the bottom of the drained lake.

"What a ride!" Average whooped.

"Let's not do it again, though." Jake paddled the makeshift boat back to shore with his bare hands. In the next boat, Rachel held onto Dr. Dave's hand with white knuckles. The Doc had a phone pressed against his ear, his face twisted in pain from her death grip.

"They're fine," Average said. "Dr. Dave is in more pain than Rachel right now."

"Follow me," he said. "I'm going after Marco."

Average leaned away like he was a live grenade. "Can't we just let the State Police deal with him?"

"He held a gun in my wife's face," Jake snarled.

"And you don't even have a weapon now!"

"He missed my pepper spray."

Average held her hands out in surrender. "Okay." She jumped from the boat into the shallow water and pushed Dr. Dave and Rachel to shore.

"Hey, look what I found!" Average held the tranq gun aloft like she was a model from a poster for Super Spy Barbie rather than a deputized waitress.

"Marco must've lost it in the tidal wave," Jake said. "It'll help."

"Your luck at work," Average said.

Jake grunted at that. "Don't like to push my luck, but I will. Just for a little longer."

"Remind me never to get on your bad side." Average held it out to him. "You want it?"

Jake held his hand out. He was a great aim, before his first wife accidentally shot herself and he swore off carrying. With the way his luck ran, he'd never really needed a gun. He let his hand fall to his side and shook his head. "You keep it.."

He ran up a trail of flattened vegetation from their tidal wave, ignoring the squishy wet sound his soaked boots made. A quarter of a mile up the mountain he spotted Professor Casari. The professor lay on his side, coughing up water. His gun lay five feet away on the ground.

He turned as Jake and Average ran toward him, then speed crawled toward the gun.

Jake took a shooter's stance with his pepper spray.

"Do you feel lucky? Because I sure do!"

Marco chewed his lip, staring at the weapon.

Average set her stance and pointed the tranq gun at him. "You won't get to it before I shoot you."

He glared at them and put his hands in the air.

Jake pulled Marco's hands behind his back and cuffed them. "When I don't want to break your nose, I'll read you your rights. Right now, I suggest you stay quiet."

Chapter 20

Average cradled the littlest Coletrane against her shoulder, humming and sending soothing feelings her way. "Not bad for twenty hours labor."

"I'm just glad for the epidural," Rachel said. She pointed with her chin at the table where Dr. Dave and Jody sat talking. "Is Doc willingly sharing a table with his ex?"

"Saying goodbyes," Average said with a shrug.

"You don't seem very concerned—for someone who just agreed to be the Doc's girl."

Average looked down at the baby. "That was just on account of Jody."

"So you two aren't going steady?" Rachel poked her in the arm.

"I wouldn't go that far." She hid a smile while smelling baby hair.

Jake watched from his stool in the diner as Michael Moder finished interviewing Sarah, shut off his camera and shook her hand.

"Headed out?" Jake asked when the documentary film maker walked by.

"I have all the footage I need now," Michael said. "We'll be in touch when the film is done and scheduled for broadcast. Between the birth of Coin's descendant, the murders, the treasure and the man eating catfish, this is not the story I envisioned. I'm still not sure how to tell it."

"I'm sure you'll get it all figured out," Jake said.

Maggie stuck her head through the doorway. "Michael? The guy who talks with a fake French accent is letting us look over all of those inventions from the Coin family vault before we leave!"

Jake whirled around. "You hired her?"

"I always need a good historian on my team. We've been one person short since Jennifer was murdered the last time we were here." Michael looked sideways at Jake. "Is that a problem?"

"No," Jake made a face. "Jody isn't interested pressing charges against her on the kidnapping. So as long as she testifies against Marco, she's free to do what she wants. Just get her out of town. She's less popular than Jody round these parts, and that's saying something."

Just then Maggie walked up. "Before I go: I know why your doctor experienced homicidal fantasies." She held up a map with writing on it for him to see. "I found this note in Sandy's work. Some subterranean pockets of gas escaped into the atmosphere when the lake drained. Anyone who breathed them would have surreal hallucinations. Your Doctor was a kind of canary in a coal mine."

Jake leaned forward in concern, ready to call Horace and argue for evacuation. Maggie held up her hands in a comforting gesture. "But don't worry, the gas is gone now."

He slumped back into his chair, mopping his brow. Then a new thought occurred to him. "Professor Caseri can't use *that* as a defense, can he?" Jake frowned.

"He could, but what jury would believe it?" Maggie's grin showed all of her teeth.

"If everyone wants to kill her, it's good *Jody's* leaving town," Jake said while at the same time giving Michael a pointed look.

"Speaking of which, where is she?" Maggie craned her neck to look around the room. "I want to be out of town before she decides we're besties."

"I think she's saying goodbye to Dr. Dave before she heads back to Memphis," Jake said in relief. He waved at a corner booth where Jody sat on one side and Dr. Dave sat as far away from her on the other as he could manage.

Maggie took one look at Jody and fled the diner.

Jody twisted her paper napkin into tiny shreds as she looked anywhere but at David. She gave him a tight, unhappy smile. "There isn't any chance I could convince you to come back with me, is there?"

David shook his head. "I've got a life here. It's not what I had in Memphis, but I'm... happy?" He blinked in surprise. "Yes, I'm happy!"

"I can see that?" Jody said. "I think you belong here, David?"

David felt a loosening in the imaginary cords that bound him up so tight that he couldn't breathe. He *did* belong.

"What will you do now?" He asked her.

"I think maybe archaeology isn't for me?" She said. "I'm going to go stay with Mother until I figure out my next step?"

"You want some advice?" David asked.

"Sure?"

"Find a place where everyone who talks sounds like they're asking a question."

Jody gave him a funny look. "Why would I do that?"

Winn, Horace and Jimbo stood around an old stock tank behind Rachel's barn. A gargantuan catfish swam in lazy circles in the tank.

"He liked those goldfish. Should we bring him some more?" Jimbo scratched his head.

"Of course he liked them," Horace said. "That's fine dining to a feller like General Custer."

Just then the catfish swam to the side of the tank and spit something out. Winn leaned down and picked it up.

"What have you got there, Winn?" Jimbo asked.

Winn held up a gold insignia ring that appeared to have the scales of justice stamped into the crest.

"Remember that lawyer fella we hired to hunt down Big Bird? I think I know what happened to him!" Winn said.

About the Author

When Tracy S. Morris isn't thinking up fun ways to kill people (for her books, we swear!) she can be found researching bonkers history for her podcast, "I Am Not Making This Up." She's an occasional radio commentator and public speaker. She lives with her husband and two kids in Springdale, Arkansas.

Tracy S. Morris

About the Artist

Brad W. Foster is an award-winning artist who has had workpublished in over a thousand books, magazines, comics, and indefinable small press publications—the man needs a hobby!

Brad has created seven covers for Yard Dog Press publications—*Illusions of Sanity*, *Wolf 's Trap*, *Hammer Town*, *Dadgum Martians Invade the Lucky Nickel Saloon*, *Fairy BrewHaHa at the Lucky Nickel Saloon*, *Jaguar Moon*, *Bride of Tranquility*, and now *It Came to Tranquility*.

Brad draws to live and finds it interesting that he also lives to draw. You can find out even more about Brad and his work at: http://www.jabberwockygraphix.com.

Yard Dog Press Titles as Of This Print Date

A Bubba in Time Saves None, Edited by Selina Rosen
A Man, A Plan, (yet lacking) A Canal, Panama, Linda Donahue
Adventures of the Irish Ninja, Selina Rosen
The Alamo and Zombies, Jean Stuntz
All the Marbles, Dusty Rainbolt
Almost Human, Gary Moreau
Ancient Enemy, Lee Killough
Angels of Mercy, Laura J. Underwood
The Anthology From Hell: Humorous Tales From WAY Down Under,
    Edited by Julia S. Mandala
Ard Magister, Laura J. Underwood
Assassins Inc., Phillip Drayer Duncan
Assassins Incorporated: Rehired, Phillip Drayer Duncan
Bad City, Selina Rosen & Laura J. Underwood
Bad Lands, Selina Rosen & Laura J. Underwood
Black Rage, Selina Rosen
Blackrose Avenue, Mark Shepherd
The Boat Man, Selina Rosen
Bobby's Troll, John Lance
Bride of Tranquility, Tracy S. Morris
Bruce and Roxanne from Start to Finnish, Rie Sheridan Rose
The Bubba Chronicles, Selina Rosen
Bubba Fables, Sue P. Sinor
Bubbas Of the Apocalypse, Edited by Selina Rosen
The Burden of the Crown, Selina Rosen
Chains of Redemption, Selina Rosen
Checking On Culture, Lee Killough
Chronicles of the Last War, Laura J. Underwood
Dadgum Martians Invade the Lucky Nickel Saloon, Ken Rand
Dark and Stormy Nights, Bradley H. Sinor
Deja Doo, Edited by Selina Rosen
Dracula's Lawyer, Julia S. Mandala
Dragon's Tongue, Laura J. Underwood
The Essence of Stone, Beverly A. Hale
Fairy BrewHaHa at the Lucky Nickel Saloon, Ken Rand
The Fantastikon: Tales of Wonder, Robin Wayne Bailey
Fire & Ice, Selina Rosen
Flush Fiction, Volume I: Stories To Be Read In One Sitting, Edited by
    Selina Rosen
Flush Fiction, Volume II: Twenty Years of Letting it Go!, Edited by
    Selina Rosen

*The Four Bubbas of the Apocalypse: Flatulence, Halitosis, Incest, and...
Ned,* Edited by Selina Rosen
The Four Redheads: Apocalypse Now!, Linda L. Donahue, Rhonda
Eudaly, Julia S. Mandala, & Dusty Rainbolt
The Four Redheads of the Apocalypse, Linda L. Donahue, Rhonda
Eudaly, Julia S. Mandala, & Dusty Rainbolt
The Four Redheads: The Wrath of Satan, Linda L. Donahue, Rhonda
Eudaly, Julia S. Mandala, & Dusty Rainbolt
The Garden in Bloom, Jeffrey Turner
The Geometries of Love: Poetry by Robin Wayne Bailey
The Golems of Laramie County, Ken Rand
The Green Women, Laura J. Underwood
The Guardians, Lynn Abbey
Hammer Town, Selina Rosen
The Happiness Box, Beverly A. Hale
The Host Series: The Host, Fright Eater, Gang Approval, Selina Rosen
Houston, We've Got Bubbas!, Edited by Selina Rosen
How I Spent the Apocalypse, Selina Rosen
I Didn't Quite Make It to Oz, Edited by Selina Rosen
I Should Have Stayed In Oz, Edited by Selina Rosen
In the Shadows, Bradley H. Sinor
International House of Bubbas, Edited by Selina Rosen
It Came to Tranquility, Tracy S. Morris
It's the Great Bumpkin, Cletus Brown!, Katherine A. Turski
Judas Gene, Gary Moreau
The Killswitch Review, Steven-Elliot Altman & Diane DeKelb-
Rittenhouse
The Leopard's Daughter, Lee Killough
The Lightning Horse, John Moore
The Logic of Departure, Mark W. Tiedemann
The Long, Cold Walk To Mars, Jeffrey Turner
Marking the Signs and Other Tales of Mischief, Laura J. Underwood
Material Things, Selina Rosen
Medieval Misfits: Renaissance Rejects, Tracy S. Morris
Mirror Images, Susan Satterfield
Mirror, Mirror and Other Reflections, James K. Burk
More Stories That Won't Make Your Parents Hurl, Edited by Selina
Rosen
Music for Four Hands, Louis Antonelli & Edward Morris
My Life with Geeks and Freaks, Claudia Christian
The Necronomicrap: A Guide to Your Horooooscope, Tim Frayser
Playing With Secrets, Bradley H & Sue P. Sinor
Redheads In Love, Linda L. Donahue, Rhonda Eudaly, Julia S.
Mandala, & Dusty Rainbolt

Reruns, Selina Rosen
Rock 'n' Roll Universe, Ken Rand
Shadows In Green, Richard Dansky
Stories That Won't Make Your Parents Hurl, Edited by Selina Rosen
Strange Robby, Selina Rosen
Tales from Keltora, Laura J. Underwood
Tales of the Lucky Nickel Saloon, Second Ave., Laramie, Wyoming, U S of A, Ken Rand
Tarbox Station, Rhonda Eudaly
Texistani: Indo-Pak Food from A Texas Kitchen, Beverly A. Hale
That's All Folks, J. F. Gonzalez
Through Wyoming Eyes, Ken Rand
Turn Left to Tomorrow, Robin Wayne Bailey
The Twins, Selina Rosen
The Undead At My Head, Ethan Nahté
Villains in Training, Julia S. Mandala and Linda L. Donahue
Wandering Lark, Laura J. Underwood
Weirdough, Inc., Selina Rosen and Sherri Dean
Wings of Morning, Katharine Eliska Kimbriel
Zombies In Oz and Other Undead Musings, Robin Wayne Bailey

Fantasy Writers Asylum (A YDP Imprint):
Blood Songs, Julia Mandala
Gateway to Corimar, Julia Mandala & Linda L Donahue
Tale of the Black Heart, Linda L. Donahue

Double Dog (A YDP Imprint):

#1:
Of Stars & Shadows, Mark W. Tiedemann
This Instance Of Me, Jeffrey Turner

#2:
Gods and Other Children, Bill D. Allen
Tranquility, Tracy Morris

#3:
Home Is the Hunter, James K. Burk
Farstep Station, Lazette Gifford

#4:
Sabre Dance, Melanie Fletcher
The Lunari Mask, Laura J. Underwood

#5:
House of Doors, Julia Mandala
Jaguar Moon, Linda A. Donahue

Just Cause (A YDP Imprint):

The Bitter End, Selina Rosen
Death Under the Crescent Moon, Dusty Rainbolt
Duckrt: Mystery at the Museum, Zeb Rosenzweig
Getting It Real, Selina Rosen
The Ghost Writer, Selina Rosen
It's Not Rocket Science: Spirituality for the Working-Class Soul, Selina
    Rosen
Meditations of a Hoarder, Melinda LaFevers
Not My Life, Selina Rosen
Permanent Solution to a Temporary Problem, Selina Rosen
The Pit, Selina Rosen
Plots and Protagonists: A Reference Guide for Writers, Mel. White
Vanishing Fame, Selina Rosen